HOMEROOM DIARIES

I make this outfit look good!
SOUND OF MIND
SCREAM OUT
We just need to love each other!
PROPERTY OF CRAZYTOWN
Yo! Yo!
Give Peace a chance!
Got the Urge to splurge!
Clothes NOT WAR
SHOE FEST
Hugs for Happiness!
Home-room Heaven!

BOOKS BY JAMES PATTERSON
FOR YOUNG ADULT READERS

For previews of upcoming books in these series and other information, visit witchandwizard.com, maximumride.com, and confessionsofamurdersuspect.com.

For more information about the author, visit jamespatterson.com.

HOMEROOM DIARIES

JAMES PATTERSON

AND LISA PAPADEMETRIOU

ILLUSTRATED BY KEINO

JIMMY Patterson Books

Little, Brown and Company

New York   Boston   London

Copyright © 2016 by James Patterson
Illustrations by Keino
Excerpt from *Cradle and All* copyright © 2016 by James Patterson
The JIMMY Patterson name and logo are trademarks of JBP Business, LLC.

JIMMY Patterson Books / Little, Brown and Company
Hachette Book Group
1290 Avenue of the Americas, New York, NY 10104
JimmyPatterson.org

First Paperback Edition: May 2016
First published in hardcover in July 2014 by Little, Brown and Company

JIMMY Patterson Books is an imprint of Little, Brown and Company, a division of Hachette
Book Group, Inc. The Little, Brown name and logo are trademarks of Hachette Book Group, Inc.

The publisher is not responsible for websites (or their content)
that are not owned by the publisher.

Library of Congress Cataloging-in-Publication Data
Patterson, James, 1947–
Homeroom diaries / by James Patterson and Lisa Papademetriou ; illustrated by Keino.—
First edition.
pages cm
Summary: Seventeen-year-old Margaret "Cuckoo" Clark keeps a journal detailing the trials and
tribulations of high school life as she and her close-knit group of outcast friends try to break down
the barriers between their school's "warring nations."
ISBN 978-0-316-20762-1 (hardcover)—ISBN 978-0-316-20763-8 (ebook)—
ISBN 978-0-316-37863-5 (international)—ISBN 978-0-316-20758-4 (paperback)
[1. High schools—Fiction. 2. Schools—Fiction. 3. Interpersonal relations—Fiction.
4. Friendship—Fiction. 5. Foster home care—Fiction. 6. Diaries—Fiction.]
I. Papademetriou, Lisa. II. Keino, illustrator. III. Title.
PZ7.P27653Hom 2014   [Fic]—dc23   2013016061

10 9 8 7 6 5 4 3 2 1

RRD-C

Printed in the United States of America

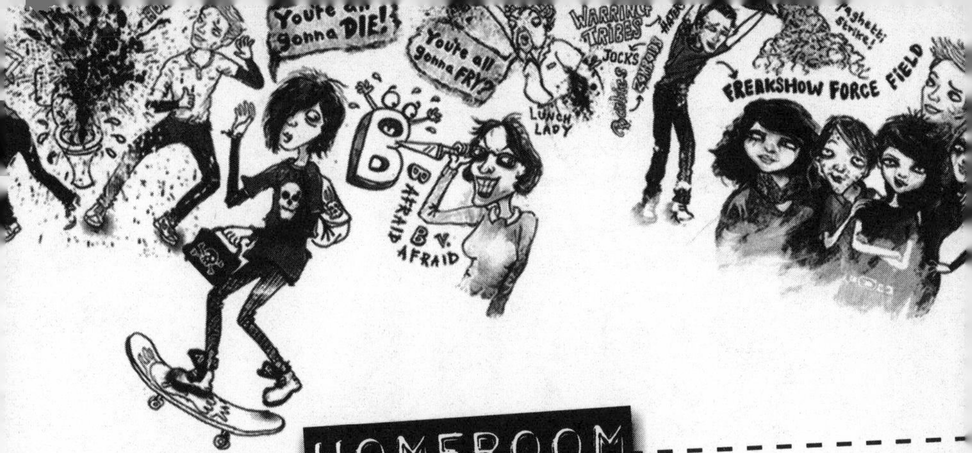
gonna DIE!
You're all gonna FRY?
B AFRAID
B V. AFRAID
LUNCH LADY
WARRING TRIBES
JOCKS
FREAKSHOW FORCE FIELD

HOMEROOM DIARIES

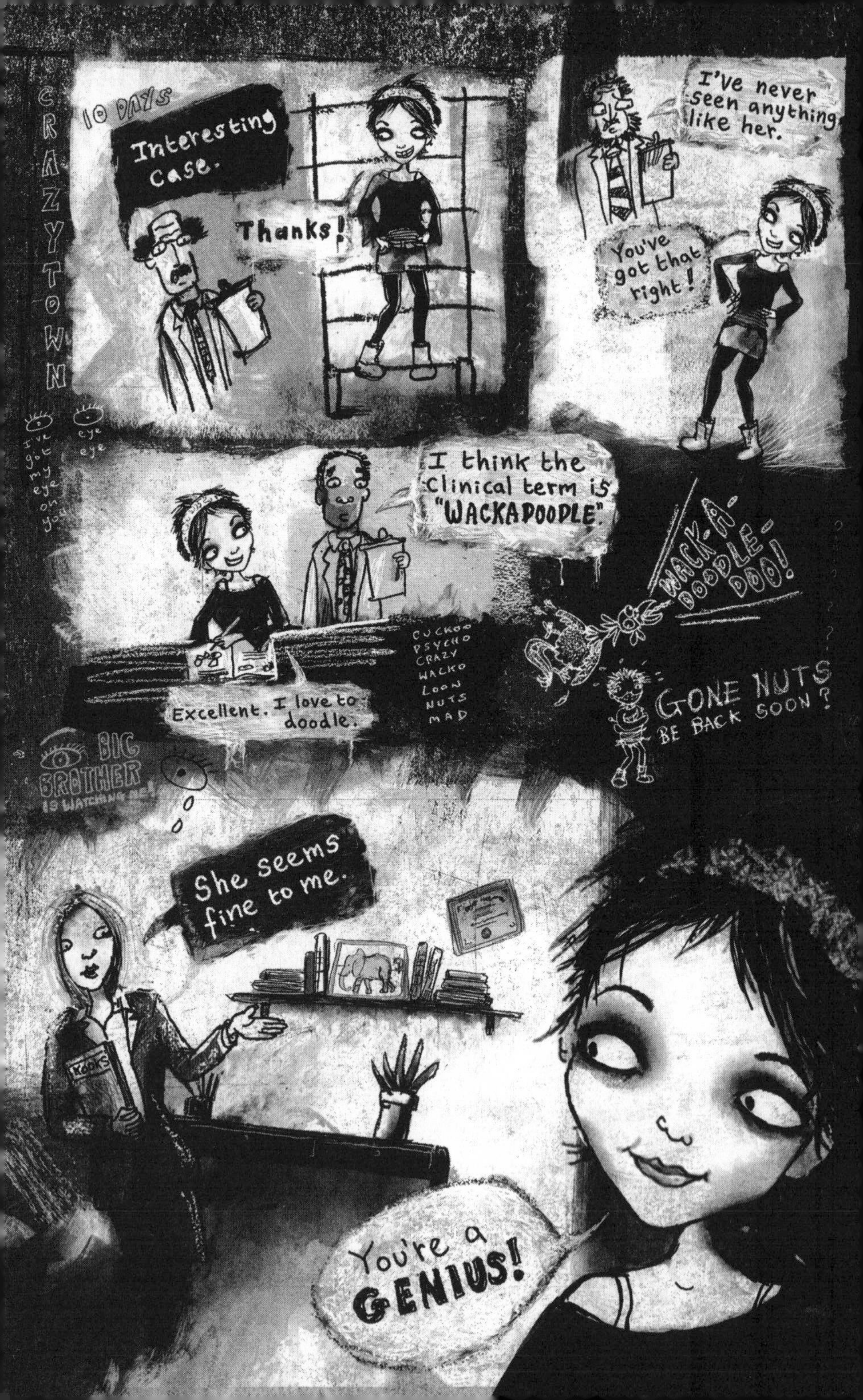
CRAZYTOWN
10 DAYS
Interesting case.
Thanks!
I've never seen anything like her.
You've got that right!
I've got my eye on you
eye eye
I think the clinical term is "WACKADOODLE".
WACK-A-DOODLE-DOO!
CUCKOO
PSYCHO
CRAZY
WACKO
LOON
NUTS
MAD
Excellent. I love to doodle.
GONE NUTS
BE BACK SOON?
BIG BROTHER
IS WATCHING ME!
She seems fine to me.
KOOKS
You're a GENIUS!

Prologue
LET'S GET HAPPY

I'm starting over.

With this diary. With everything.

So welcome to it.

And if we're going to be friends—and I know we are—then I might as well be completely straight with you. I mean, what kind of person lies in her own diary? There's something I need to get out of the way before we get any further.

I started this diary as a patient at "Crazytown." That's what us locals call the psych ward at St. Augustine Community Hospital in Portland, Oregon, where I went for a ten-day "observation period" not too long ago.

Look, before you jump on the pity train and start thinking that this is going to be one of those god-awful books where the "big reveal" is that the girl goes nuts and a lot of her quirky, lovable friends in the asylum go berserk and try to kill her, let me just say that It Wasn't That Bad. People were actually really nice to me. In fact, everyone found me fascinating!

In other words, they observed me. And I observed me, too. It was all very observational. They were trying to make sure I wasn't going to hurt myself, and I was trying to figure out why

I had spent the last three months crying absolutely all the time and at the most embarrassing moments possible, like at my friend Katie's house while we were watching *Bridesmaids*. I mean, I completely lost it when Melissa McCarthy pooped in the sink. Katie started to get really concerned then because that is not like me. At all.

Does that sound sane to you?

But after ten days in Crazytown, I finally decided that I wasn't too much crazier than most kids I know. I was just furious—mostly at my mom, who disappeared one Tuesday afternoon without a word or even a good-bye kiss.

For a while, I worried that something horrible had happened to her. Then I worried that nothing had happened and she just decided to leave. I still don't know the answer, which can definitely make someone a certain kind of crazy (we're talking squirrel-stuck-in-a-storm-drain freak-out).

But I am feeling a lot better now. I'm working on Getting Happy. My best friend, Katie, has been doing a lot of reading on happiness lately—like, books on how to Get Happy. (Yes, there are instruction manuals.) Some of the books say you should challenge yourself and try new things. Writing in my diary is supposed to help, too.

Now that I have been certified "sound of mind," things are really looking up.

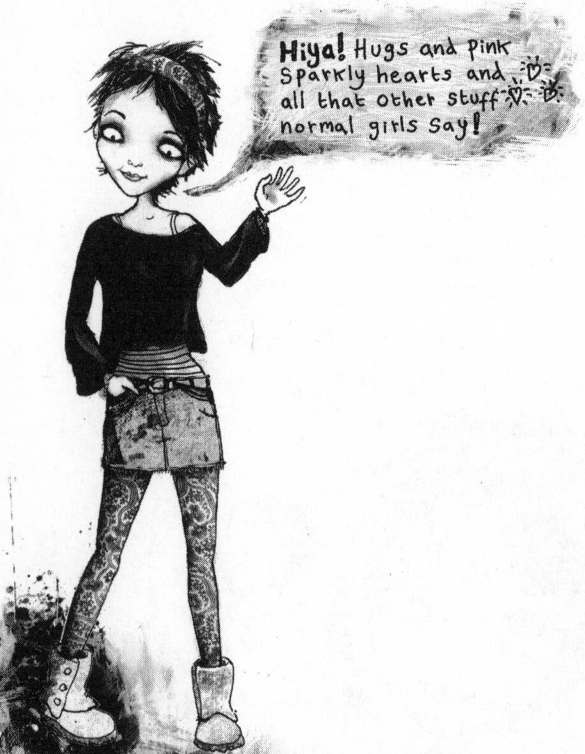
Hiya! Hugs and pink sparkly hearts and all that other stuff normal girls say!

I'm Cuckoo Clarke.

This story mostly takes place in a small town outside Portland called North Plains. There's a gun shop outside town that has an annual Back-to-School Sale. (I'm anti-gun.) Every August, our town hosts the World's Largest Elephant Garlic Festival. (I'm pro-garlic.) Most people around here wear Nikes, Portland's proudest. (I prefer Uggs, but I wouldn't say I'm definitely pro- or anti-footwear.)

And now, welcome to the main setting of this show: North Plains High School! It looks the way you're probably picturing it.

The hallways are full of the Usual Suspects: Jocks, Nerds, Twinkies, Otaku, Barbies, Goths, Eurotrash, Jailbait, Stoners, Joiners, Glommers, Delusionals, Haters, Wankstas, Thespians, Teachers, Terror Teachers, Zomboids, Robots, Gleeks, United Colors of Benettoners, Libertarians, Activists, Juvies, Baristas, Blahs, and—my best friends—the Freakshow.

That's right. We call ourselves the Freakshow. My best friend, Brainzilla (Katie), had this idea that we should give our little group a nickname that's *far worse* than anything any of the diseased minds in our school could dream up.

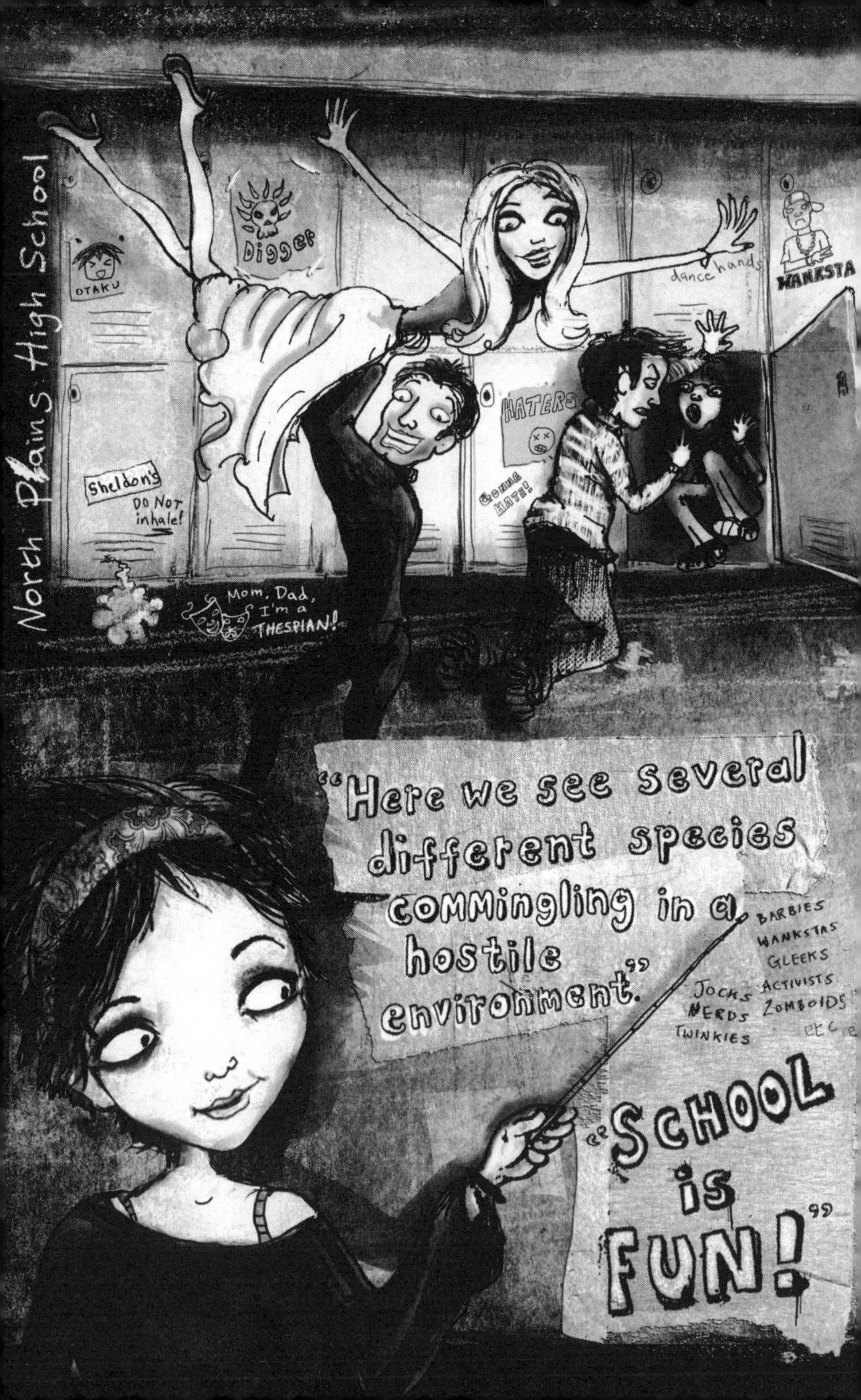
North Plains High School
OTAKU
Digger
dance hands
WANKSTA
Sheldon's
DO NOT inhale!
HATERS
GONNA HATE!
Mom, Dad, I'm a THESPIAN!
"Here we see several different species commingling in a hostile environment."
BARBIES
WANKSTAS
GLEEKS
ACTIVISTS
JOCKS
NERDS
ZOMBOIDS
TWINKIES
etc
"SCHOOL is FUN!"

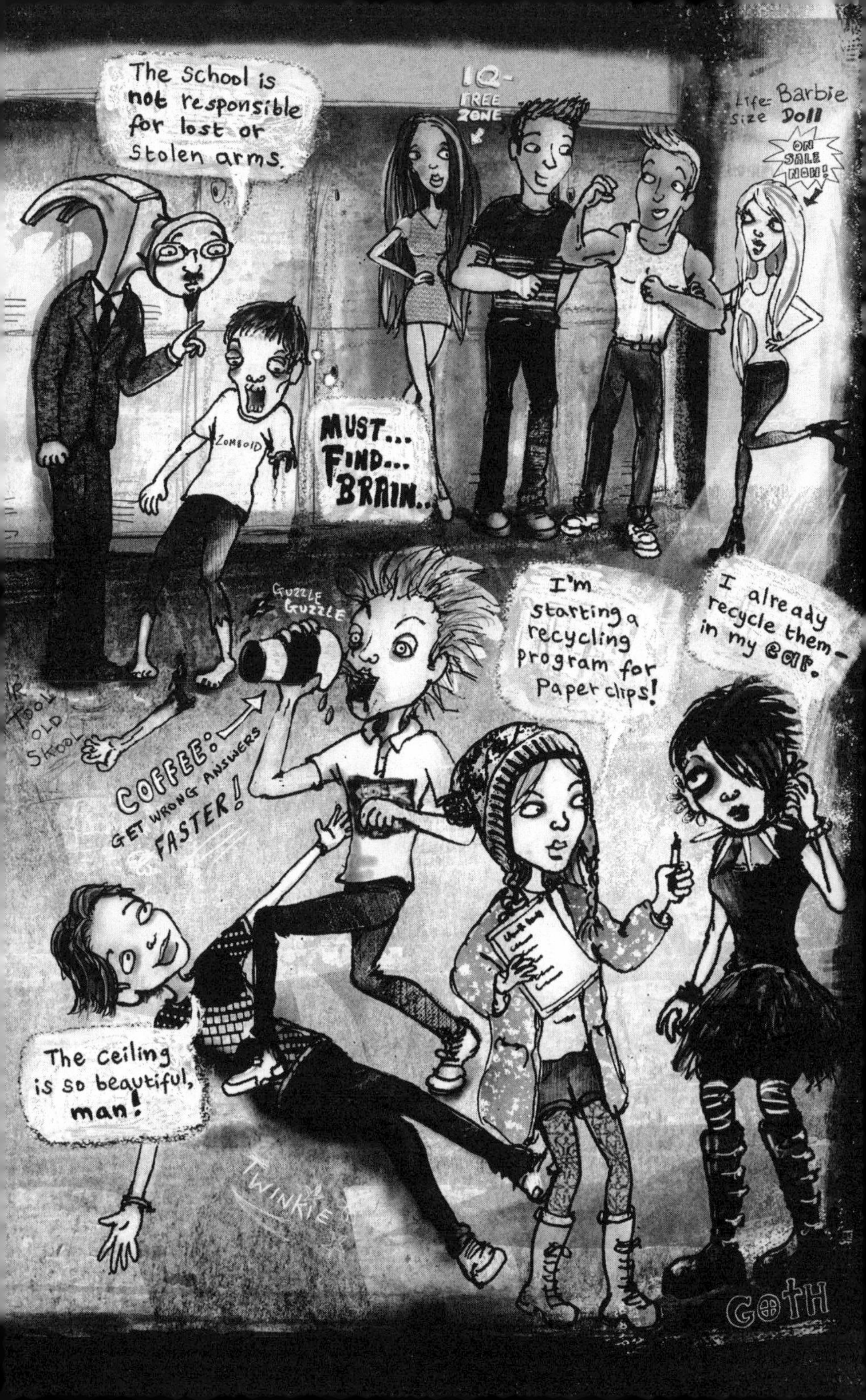
The School is not responsible for lost or stolen arms.
IQ-FREE ZONE
Life-Size Barbie Doll
ON SALE NOW!
ZOMBOID
MUST... FIND... BRAIN..
TOO OLD SKOOL
GUZZLE GUZZLE
COFFEE: GET WRONG ANSWERS FASTER!
I'm starting a recycling program for Paper clips!
I already recycle them—in my ear.
The ceiling is so beautiful, man!
TWINKIE
GOTH

Don't most high schools smell/look/sound the same?

Anyway, after the Freakshow was born, we actually took it a step further and gave ourselves insulting individual nicknames, too. I think we did a pretty good job with them:

Brainzilla is number one in our class. She's IB (that's International Baccalaureate) and determined to be the first person in her family to go to college. She has set her sights on Yale and has even already scheduled an interview—two years early. She works her butt off constantly and then goes home to take care of her three little brothers. Her parents work weird shifts, so her house is messy and complicated and basically covered in snot.

Hana named herself Eggroll ("Eggy" for short) after a couple of racist creeps asked her about her "dumplings." She has about a thousand interests, but sadly for her parents, school isn't one of them. Paul has zits everywhere that I know about, so "Zitsy" was an easy choice. He's deathly afraid he'll end up working in his father's plumbing business. Peter covers us with both the jocks and the Religious Right, so "Tebow" seemed like a good fit. He's also insanely good looking. Flatso, formerly Beverly, is overweight, but also flat breasted, which is rare and borderline tragic. She happens to be strong enough to rip your head off. Not that she would. She's the sweetest person I know.

And then there's me, Cuckoo.

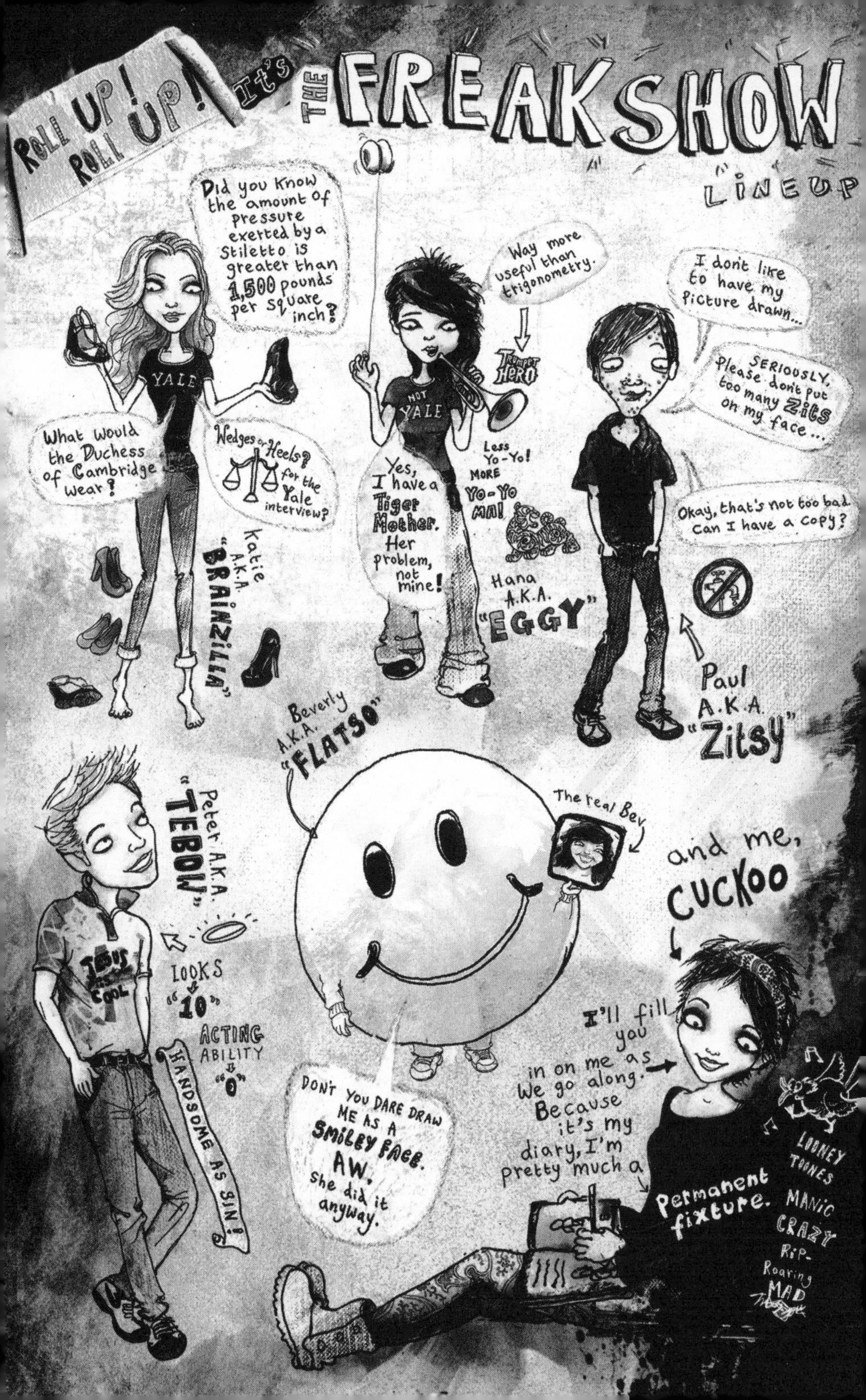

ROLL UP! ROLL UP! It's THE FREAKSHOW LINEUP
Did you know the amount of pressure exerted by a Stiletto is greater than 1,500 pounds per square inch?
What would the Duchess of Cambridge wear?
Wedges or Heels? for the Yale interview?
YALE
Katie A.K.A. "BRAINZILLA"
Way more useful than trigonometry.
TRUMPET HERO
NOT YALE
Less Yo-Yo! MORE YO-YO MA!
Yes, I have a Tiger Mother. Her problem, not mine!
Hana A.K.A. "EGGY"
I don't like to have my picture drawn...
SERIOUSLY. Please don't put too many ZITS on my face...
Okay, that's not too bad. Can I have a copy?
Paul A.K.A. "Zitsy"
Beverly A.K.A. "FLATSO"
The real Bev
Peter A.K.A. "TEBOW"
JESUS IS COOL
LOOKS "10"
ACTING ABILITY "0"
HANDSOME AS SIN!
DON'T YOU DARE DRAW ME AS A SMILEY FACE.
AW, she did it anyway.
and me, CUCKOO
I'll fill you in on me as we go along. Because it's my diary, I'm pretty much a permanent fixture.
LOONEY TOONES
MANIC
CRAZY
RIP-Roaring MAD

So now you've met the whole gang. You'd think with the zillion other cliques, clubs, and posses in this place that we'd all fit in somewhere, but we don't. The truth is that this school is a mess of warring nations. Jocks hate Nerds. Barbies hate Goths. Blah blah blah. But my friends and I are planning to do something about that.

It's Monday, and it's raining, so the hallways are wet as we all drag in droplets on our shoes and clothes.

Digger Whitlock gives me a cheerful hello as he passes by my locker.

His family owns the local funeral parlor. They specialize in Vegas-glitz coffin interiors, and Digger's dad will—for an extra two hundred bucks—dress up as Elvis and sing "Love Me Tender" at your beloved's interment. So he's allowed to be a little messed up.

And there's also this: Digger's older brother died in a car crash last year. He had a beautiful coffin. But even so, it gives me the shivers to think about Andy Whitlock. I really hate the idea of being dead. (Although I love sleeping, so I'm not sure what that's about.)

I think I just hate endings in general. They're so…final.

Maybe that's another reason I'm starting this diary. I'm a big fan of beginnings. Especially beginnings—and second chances.

And short chapters, obviously. So, I think you get the picture. Of me. Of my friends. Of North Plains High School.

Basically, it's like being back in the asylum.

With more homework.

Chapter 2
HOW TO SURVIVE HOMEROOM
(AND THE REST OF THE DAY)

I'm sitting in homeroom scribbling and surviving.

I was reading *Pride and Prejudice* a minute ago, and I'm really into the book. I just love that Janie Austen.

Now I'm imagining myself meeting a boy in my *personal* version of *Pride and Prejudice*. His name is Laurence Darcy, and he's the younger brother of Fitzwilliam Darcy, better known as Mr. Darcy, and he is just so charming and British and Jane Austen-y that it's like I'm in homeroom heaven!

We start chatting at a society ball at Netherfield Park.

Laurence Darcy is pretty dreamy. I'm just loving all those great nineteenth-century manners!

Hmm. I may be in love. Stay tuned.

Laurence Darcy gets me through the rest of homeroom and, let's face it, the rest of my classes, until lunchtime.

Hold your fire, Teachers, Barbies, and all Haters, I think as I walk through the cafeteria doors. I'm immediately hit in the face with the greasy, smelly reminder that the caf offers almost nothing that hasn't taken a long and luxurious bath in the FryDaddy. It's sick. The Activists are lobbying for a salad bar, and I say, "Dare to dream, Activists!" I really love their hopeful energy and vision for a brighter tomorrow!

Today I take my brown bag over to the Freakshow Corner. That's the table where my biffles and I sit every day. It has a good view of the parking lot.

When I get there, I see a Hater—Marty Bloom—trying to shove something into Zitsy's face. Zitsy's trying to get away, but his head is pulled way back, and I'm worried that his neck might snap like a rubber band.

"Come on! You freaks usually can't keep your pieholes shut!" Marty says.

"Get away from him, Marty," I say. Zitsy has been pushed around so much that he doesn't even fight back anymore. He says he's used to it, but I'm not. I really hate it. "Leave him alone!"

Marty backs off, surprise curving his straight black eyebrows.

"I was just fooling around." He punches Zitsy in the arm. Maybe he means it to be playful, but Zitsy winces. "What's the big deal, Maggie?"

"I'm Cuckoo, remember?" I tell him. "And Zitsy's my friend. Don't touch."

"Compassion and respect, people!" Eggy pipes up as she walks up behind me.

"What she said," I agree.

"That's what Jesus would do," Tebow puts in, which is a little over the top, but not completely wrong, either. He sits down next to Zitsy so Marty won't try anything again.

Marty narrows his eyes. "That right there is what makes people want to mash pie in your face," he snaps, and walks off. "You owe me three bucks for the food," he calls back over his shoulder to Zitsy, then cracks up.

Zitsy looks down at the plate that's sitting on the table in front of him. "I hate pie," he says quietly. Eggy hands him a pile of napkins, and he starts wiping gooey peach from his face.

Flatso has joined us now, and she wraps her thick arms around Zitsy. Then Eggy does, then Tebow, then me.

"Is everything okay?" Brainzilla asks as she walks over to join us. "Why are we all hugging?" She doesn't wait for an answer. She just puts down her tray and joins in.

And that is why I love my friends. Because they aren't afraid to create a Human Hug-Blob in the middle of the cafeteria, even if it means getting stared at.

Chapter 3
DEPRIVED

After what seems like ten years but is still too short to me, we stop hugging and get back to our seats. Fifteen minutes left in lunch. Plenty of time, as long as we skip chewing and go for the direct-food-inhale.

"Okay, so that hug gave me a new idea," Eggy announces.

"For Operation Happiness?" Brainzilla guesses, and Eggy nods.

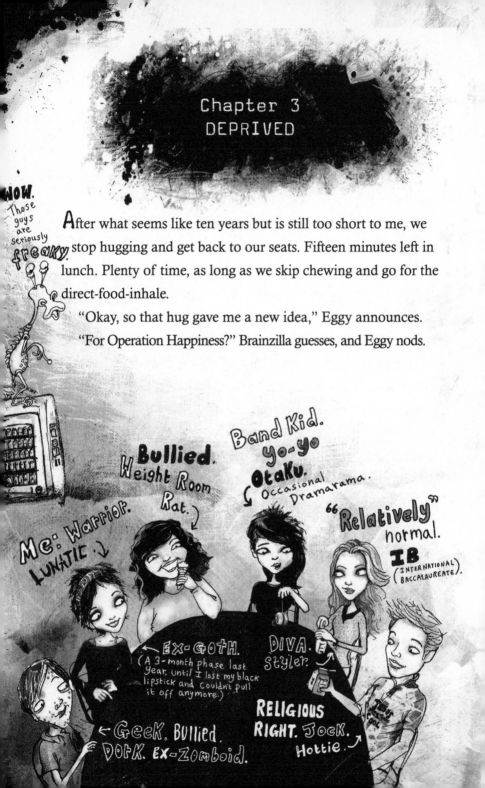

WOW. Those guys are seriously freaky.

Me: Warrior. LUNATIC ↓

Bullied. Weight Room Rat. ↓

Band Kid. yo-yo Otaku. ↓ Occasional Dramarama.

"Relatively" normal. IB (INTERNATIONAL BACCALAUREATE).

← EX-GOTH. (A 3-month phase last year, until I lost my black lipstick and couldn't pull it off anymore.)

DIVA. Styler. →

← Geek. Bullied. DorK. EX-Zomboid.

RELIGIOUS RIGHT. Jock. Hottie. →

"Okay, so the idea is called Hands Across the Football Field," Eggy says.

"I already love it," Flatso gushes.

"The whole school would join hands for five minutes," Eggy says, and I look at her like she's the one who's cuckoo.

Zitsy seems into it, though, and leans forward. "And then what?"

"Maybe pass a squeeze back and forth," Eggy adds. Wow. It's so…over the top.

"Um—" I start, but Zitsy interrupts.

"I think the key here is snacks."

"I wasn't thinking snacks," Eggy admits.

"Either way, it definitely has potential," Brainzilla says, but Tebow shakes his head.

"Coach Struthers hates having civilians out on 'his' turf," he says. "He'll get the whole team to chase us off."

It's true. Coach Struthers is a nut about the turf. Once I went to watch Tebow practice, and when I stepped on one of the chalk lines, I got whistle-blasted loud enough to cause brain damage.

Yep. That's just one example of the tragicomedy that is North Plains High.

It's kind of like *Hamlet* meets *Bridesmaids*.

I watch Zitsy push his bag of vinegar chips around, not eating them. That's not like him. Usually he eats so fast and so much that it's like watching a wood chipper. Zitsy not eating is bumming me out.

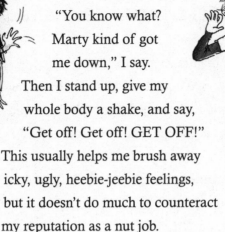

"You know what? Marty kind of got me down," I say. Then I stand up, give my whole body a shake, and say, "Get off! Get off! GET OFF!" This usually helps me brush away icky, ugly, heebie-jeebie feelings, but it doesn't do much to counteract my reputation as a nut job.

"Why does Marty have to be such a Hater, anyway?" Flatso asks, not really expecting an answer.

But I surprise Flatso with my response. "Because"—I give her a grin—"he's *deprived*."

"Hellz yeah," says Eggy, and Tebow crows, "It's on!"

"Oh, boy." Brainzilla puffs out a breath that lifts her bangs from her forehead. "Here we go."

Yeah, that's right—it's time for another round of our favorite game: DEPRIVED!

Goal: To be the object of greatest pity.

How to Play: State a way in which your life has been hideously deprived.

In the end, we declare Zitsy the winner.

He spends the last ten seconds of lunch vacuuming chips and high-octane Coke into his digestive system.

That's when I know that my friend is all right.

DEPRIVED!

CUCKOO

Because of her guardian's dairy allergy, Cuckoo is deprived of **Cheese!**

Please, Sir, may I have a crumb of cheddar?

Denied! You ARE... **DEPRIVED!**

FLATSO

Because of a lack of funds, **Flatso** is deprived of a membership at the fancy gym! She'll never win a gold medal in weight lifting‼

I'll never get to be on a box of **Wheaties!**

TEBOW

Because of a recent football-related finger injury compounded by a painful hangnail, **Tebow** has zero chance of a future as a hand model. (Probably not deprived of a future as a **Calvin Klein** Underwear model, though, if we're being honest.)

I'll never be a concert pianist! I'm **SO** deprived!

ZITSY

Because his father is a plumber, **Zitsy** is deprived of the blissful ignorance of the contents of most people's drains.

The horror, the horror! Return me to a state of ignorant bliss!

EGGY

Eggy's parents have plenty of money but don't believe in paying for cable! **Deprived!**

Eggy! Do your homework!

KNOCK!
KNOCK!

Do more!

I already did it!

But I'll never know if Honey Boo Boo wins the pageant!

BRAINZILLA

Clotheshorse **Katie** is deprived of having a legitimate excuse to buy a **Vera Wang** wedding dress.

Do I really need to have a wedding? Couldn't I just wear it to school? Or Prom?

Chapter 4
LOVE AND BIO

We interrupt this diary for an announcement: There's a new kid in bio!

He's just standing at the front of the room scanning the class with his big blue eyes, like maybe he can't decide where to sit. He chews on a fingernail, adorably nervous. I'm still all about Operation Happiness, so I walk right up to him and introduce myself.

"Welcome to North Plains High School!" I say. "We're all about helping each other here. Our motto is 'We're in this together!'" (Actually, our motto is "Educating students to succeed in a changing world," but that sounds kind of ominous to me. Mine's better.)

"Um, thanks." An awkward laugh stumbles from his lips. "Uh—do you want to take a seat?"

"Oh, sure, but I already have a lab partner." I wave my finger at Flatso, who is sitting at our black marble lab table with her notebook open and pen poised.

"Helleeeeew!" Flatso calls in an inexplicably English accent.

"Okay, well, why don't you go sit down," New Kid says, which strikes me as a little weird. But I assume he thinks maybe we'll have more time to hang out after class, so I head over to my seat.

"He's absolutely darling!" Flatso whispers.

"Why are you suddenly British?" I whisper back.

"Don't you think it makes me sound more refined?" she asks as the New Kid walks up to the front of the room and *starts the class*.

Yes, that's right—he's not the New Kid. He's the *New Teacher*!

I can feel my science grade drop out from under me.

"Um, hello. I'm Winston Quinn." He starts to write it on the board, and the chalk gives off a deafening screech. "Heh," he says, and starts again, but then the chalk breaks. He scrambles underneath his desk to get it, and when he pops back up, his face is pink. He takes a deep breath and says, "Well, anyway, you can all call me Winnie."

"What happened to Ms. Donaldson?" Langston Connors shouts from the back of the room.

"Uh—I'm not—" Winnie blushes deeper, and sweeps his blond bangs out of his eyes. I swear, he looks like he's sixteen. "I'm not actually at liberty to discuss it."

That sets the whole room off.

"Um, could everybody…could you all…settle down, please," Winnie says, sort of waving his hands a little bit.

He's never going to get anywhere with that, I think. I feel pretty bad for him as he sits down behind his desk and nervously looks at his watch. Then he starts scanning the room again, but I realize he's not just looking at the students. He's studying the walls, the desks, even the ceiling, like he's never been inside a regular old classroom before.

The room is still going strong with theories, but the main points for now are she's not coming back, Winnie is our new teacher, and the front row no longer needs to worry about Ms. Donaldson's rampant spittle problem.

Meanwhile, beside me, I can see Flatso falling madly in love.

I'm not the kind of person who gets crushes on teachers, but I can absolutely see where she's coming from. He's definitely working the cute cherub look with his pink cheeks and punk preppy haircut.

I try to picture Flatso and Winnie out on a date. Where would they go? The gym first, then the natural science museum?

Winnie eventually gets everyone calmed down and calls the roll, and when he says, "Margaret Clarke?" I raise my hand and say, "Everyone calls me Cuckoo."

He gives me a dimply smile. "All right, if you insist. Cuckoo it is."

"Her friends call her Kooks," Flatso chimes in. Still English.

"So noted, Kooks." And he actually *writes that down*. I'm starting to suspect that Winston Quinn might be extremely cool.

When I get home, Mrs. Morris is waiting for me with a plate of cookies. I feel like I'm six years old again…except that nobody ever had cookies waiting for me when I was six. But here they are, freshly baked and delicious! Mrs. Morris is my foster mom, and I love her, and she loves me, but we never really get into it like that.

I'm really touched that she went to all the trouble of baking me cookies, and when she heads toward the fridge to get me some soy milk, I leap out of my chair.

"I'll do it, Mrs. Morris," I tell her. I don't want her to go to any trouble.

How was your day?

Wonderful.

Cookies

I love musicals!

Well, Digger was his usual insane self, then Marty bullied Zitsy, so the FREAKSHOW had a group hug and came up with this awesome idea that totally won't work, and I've got a new teacher who seems really nice, but Mrs. Rosewater and Ms. Olsson are still on my back, and I think I may have come up with an idea for a new ending to Twilight, but I'm not sure that a musical number would work. …

Yeah, I call her Mrs. Morris. She once asked me to call her Roberta, but I just...couldn't. I think she was actually kind of relieved. That's just how we roll.

Mrs. Morris has a sweet, old, floppy little dog named Morris the Dog. She says there used to be a famous Morris the Cat on TV. Morris looks kind of like a mop, handle removed. Maybe he's got that in his bloodline.

Mrs. Morris also has a daughter, Marjorie, who is a total flake blowing around in the LA smog. She's a wannabe actress/singer/songwriter/screenwriter working as a barista/telemarketing trainee.

can also be used for Swiffering!

more Pink

Pink, Pink, Pink

Is my triple-shot, half-caf, skinny, no-foam cappuccino ready yet ??

Marjorie Medusa hair!

Hi, my name is Marjorie Morris, and I'm calling to update your bank card — but first let me tell you about my screenplay. I'm calling from LA, by the way. Los Angeles? I'm not calling from Mumbai, or some city in Arizona. Oh, sorry — I didn't realize this was a Phoenix area code. Anyway...

Marjorie calls just before dinner tonight. I answer the phone, and her voice clues me in right away that something's up. "Oh, uh, I don't think she's available right now," I mutter, but Mrs. Morris's got some kind of Sixth Marjorie Sense ("I hear flaky people!") and says, "Is that my daughter?" so I hand over the phone.

"Marjorie!" Mrs. Morris says into the receiver with a smile that practically reaches around to the back of her head. "We can't wait to see you—what's that? Oh. Uh-huh." Mrs. Morris's smile drops right off her face and onto the floor, splattering there. "I see. No, of course I understand. Of course. All right, Marjorie, well, another time, then...." And she clicks the off button and carefully places the phone back in its cradle.

The silence in the kitchen is like something you could swim in. "She's not coming next weekend?"

Mrs. Morris takes a deep breath. "Not this time," she says. "She wants to pick up an extra shift or two to cover her rent. Well! When the screenplay sells, she won't have to worry anymore, will she?" Then Mrs. Morris starts whistling, which is how I know she's really, really disappointed.

Morris the Dog snorts.

I barely know Marjorie...but I know I really hate her for always breaking Mrs. Morris's heart.

Chapter 6
MEET HOLDEN CAULFIELD

Mrs. Morris fries up some eggs and sausage for one of our incredibly early dinners, and I help by making dairy-free pancakes. We pretend we're running a diner, serving up two Number Six Lumberjack Breakfast platters. I even class up the plates by adding some apple slices for a garnish.

"Verna—bus Table Eleven!" Mrs. Morris says when we're finished eating.

"I'm on it, Trixie!" I load up the dishwasher and wipe down the table with a rag. Then, because I'm in a diner, I place the chairs upside down on the table and sweep the floor. While I'm at it, I mop. Why not?

"Well! The health inspector will be mighty glad to see this," Mrs. Morris says, beaming at the shiny floor. It makes me happy to make her happy.

I head up to my room to start rereading *The Catcher in the Rye* for class. Ms. Olsson would probably freak out if I ever told her, but I never study for English. Instead, I just read all the books twice. The first time through, I read in a rush because I'm always dying to find out what happens and make sure everyone's okay in the end. The second time around, I really get to enjoy the book, and I always notice new things.

When I walk through my bedroom door, I see that Holden Caulfield is sitting at my desk. Well, I'm just imagining him, but still. He's watching me, and when I say, "Hi," he says, "Hi. What are you doing in my room?"

That's a little disconcerting, but when I look around, I notice the Pencey Prep pennant on the wall instead of my Nicki Minaj poster and the hardwood floors instead of the pink carpeting that runs throughout Mrs. Morris's house. We *are* in his room!

What are you doing in my room?

Holden! It's so great to meet you! I love The Catcher in the Rye - especially the clever, sometimes-whiny voice in your head!

You can hear the voice in my head?

"How's your sister, Phoebe?" I ask.

"She's got the grippe, but I think she'll be fine. How's Mrs. Morris?"

I'm *thrilled* that he knows about Mrs. Morris! "She's great!" I say, sitting down on the bed. "Well, more like okay. You know, her MS bothers her. It gives her the shakes sometimes. She has to use a walker, and sometimes a wheelchair. And her heart is a little jumpy."

I bite my lip. I really hate talking about Mrs. Morris's health. It freaks me out a little. "Hey—while I have you here—could you help me out with some homework?"

I make up something about "coming of age" and "loss of innocence" and scribble it in my notebook. I try to use vocabulary that Ms. Olsson likes. You know: *ostracize* and *liberate* and *innocuous* and blahdeblahblah.

"Are you all right, Cuckoo?" Holden asks after a moment. "I'm worried."

Holden has plenty of his own stuff to worry about—he doesn't need to pile my problems on top of his. "Well, to tell the truth, Holden, I'm worried about you, too."

Holden sucks in his breath, like I just tossed water on him. He sighs and rubs his hand over the million little short gray hairs on the side of his head. With soft eyes, he asks, "Will I be okay?"

I really want to say yes, but I just don't know. It's kind of hard to tell from the way the book ends. So instead I say, "I sure hope so, Holden. You're one of my all-time favorite book characters." I scoot to the edge of my bed and give him a light kiss on the cheek.

He smiles a little, but the sadness remains in his eyes. I reach for his hand, and we sit there for a while, not speaking. Finally, I open my (or I guess *his*) book and start reading, and when I look up, he's gone.

I wonder if the ending of *The Catcher in the Rye* will be different this time. Whenever I reread something, especially if the ending is sad, I always kind of hope that there will be a new, perfectly happy ending on the last page.

For instance, I'm currently working on a new way to wrap up the Twilight books. I have to admit, I loved all of them. If that makes me *so* 2012, then so be it.

Chapter 7
CLUBBING

Oh, don't mind me, I'm just heading out to the country club. Why, yes, I do like to spend a great deal of time there. No, I don't play tennis; I mostly spend my time at the restaurant. It's ever so droll!

Sorry. I start talking like that whenever I go to the club for work. It's completely involuntary and usually only stops when Brainzilla starts mocking me.

We take the bus to the club whenever they need us, which is a lot during their busy seasons and not so much the rest of the time. But, hey, we'll take what we can get.

The city bus huffs up in a cloud of carbon monoxide and belches to a stop. "Here." Brainzilla is waiting with me, and I hand her two crisp dollar bills.

borrowed from Princess Kate

"How did you know?" she asks, tucking her long blond hair behind her ear. Brainzilla is one of the prettiest girls in school, and a total clotheshorse. She spends every spare cent on clothes and is, therefore, always short for the bus.

Cranberry juice

You should come sometime! The country club is soooo delightful!

My best friend blushes and says, "Sorry I'm short, but this scarf was on sale—"

"It's great. Just hit me back on the way home out of your tips." Brainzilla always makes a killing at the club. Gorgeousness + excellent manners = serious cash. The cash I earn is much less serious.

When we arrive, we're greeted by two kinds of people: people who work there and people who play there. The people who play there are mostly okay, but I always feel a little dingy around them. They're shiny. Shiny, shiny people. Their teeth are white and even, and their skin is all glowy, and their clothes always look brand-new.

The people who work there are like me and Brainzilla. You know—kinda deprived. Mostly broke.

Cuckoo:

Trimmed by Mrs. Morris over the kitchen sink.

When nutty, sent to Crazytown.

Purchased at Carl's Crazee Dealz!

Main fashion accessory: rag.

Held together with duct tape.

Random Shiny Person:

Trimmed by Hollywood stylist.

When nutty, sent to luxury rehab at The Sanctuary.

Purchased in Paris, at a boutique too fancy to have a name.

Main fashion accessory: iPhone Titanium (not yet available to public)

Nike Alphas, perfect for running to catch helicopter rides.

Usually, I start out doing prep for the kitchen, but when the main floor gets busy, I waitress with Brainzilla. So once I've set up all the garnishes, I grab my pad and pencil and head out to Table 16 where—surprise!—Marty Bloom is waiting for me with his entire family.

Actually, it's interesting to see Marty here, instead of at school. His little sister leans against him, like she thinks that he's the greatest big brother ever. His mom is very smiley, and his dad is the kind of guy who seems to always be clapping everyone on the back. They seem really nice, and when they place their order, Marty's mom apologizes for wanting her sauce on the side, which I think is cute.

So this raises the question. *Why such a Hater, Marty Bloom?*

I'm about to head over to check on Table 4 with a pitcher of water, when I nearly run into Marty, who is headed for the men's room. "Hey, Maggie," Marty says. "You look pretty."

I stop, too surprised to say "thank you" or even "my name is Cuckoo," while he doesn't even break his stride—just heads right into the restroom, as if giving me a compliment is the most natural thing in the world.

I don't know what to make of it. Is it a sign of remorse for torturing Zitsy? A sign of an imminent zombie apocalypse?

Or maybe just a sign that I look relatively cute in a black skirt and apron?

I make this uniform look g@@d.

cute—for a townie.

CATWALK CUCKOO

The next day at school is a red-letter day: Tater Tot day at lunch! Of course I get some, then grab some juice and follow Zitsy toward our table. He's got a tray loaded down with two Cokes, a slab of meat, and a mountain of fried starch—french fries, Tater Tots, two bags of chips.

We pass by the Hater table, and I shoot Marty a smile. He smiles back, then shifts in his chair, and before I know what has happened, Zitsy goes flying, his tray doing a triple somersault in midair. A rain of starch and Coke splatters all over Jenna McClue—head Barbie and on-off-on girlfriend of Marty Bloom. She lets out a screech one second before Zitsy's meat loaf lands with a thwack on her chest region. And approximately one nanosecond later, the lunchroom erupts into food fight chaos.

"Everybody, listen up!" Tebow shouts. The cafeteria quiets down as people stop throwing stuff and stop to look up at him. "Look, I know this is fun, but...it's wrong to waste food when there are starving people in the world."

Tebow is always thinking about poor people, even when people around him are tossing mashed potatoes in one another's faces. It's sweet that he cares, although I'm not sure anybody else does.

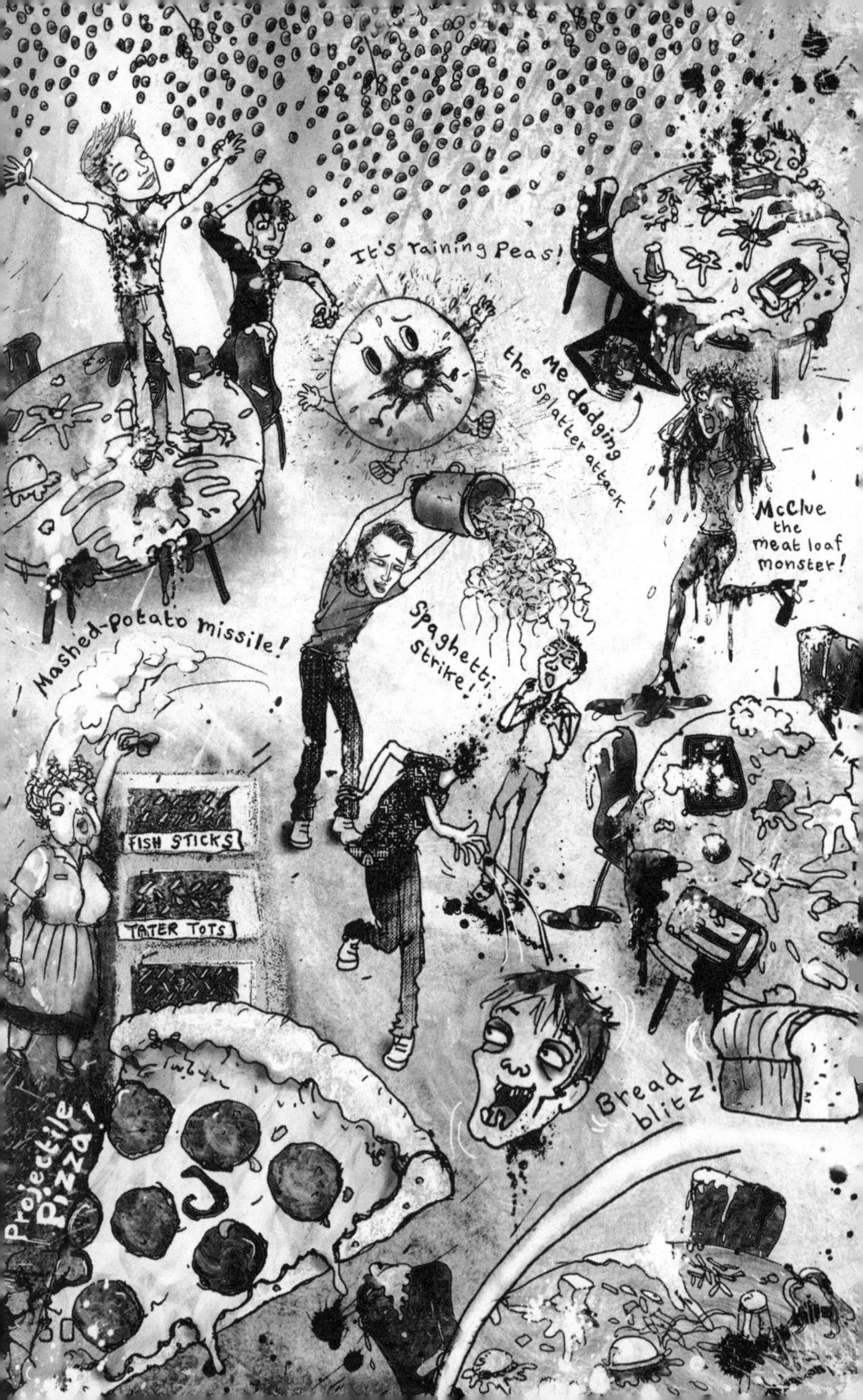
It's raining Peas!
Me dodging the Splatter attack
McClue the meat loaf monster!
Spaghetti strike!
Mashed-Potato missile!
FISH STICKS
TATER TOTS
Bread blitz!
Projectile Pizza!

"Wouldn't we all feel better if we shared what we have instead of throwing it at each other?" Tebow asks. "Wouldn't it be—"

Yes, that's a chili dog that just smacked into Tebow's forehead. The minute it hits him, the cafeteria cheers and everyone goes back to flinging food.

"Was I really being that annoying?" Tebow asks as he pulls a kidney bean out of his blond hair.

"*Never!*" Flatso insists loyally just as Zitsy says, "Yeah, dude—totally."

Tebow looks at me to break the tie. "Not everything is a 'What Would Jesus Do?' moment,"
I point out.

Some kind of green substance splats against the side of Eggy's head. "Ew!" she shrieks, and before I know it, she has flung my Tater Tots at the jock table.

Zitsy grabs two squirt bottles of ketchup and squeezes them all over the jock table. One of the Barbies comes after Brainzilla, who tosses a glass of fruit punch in the girl's face. Even Tebow starts hurling fried tofu squares like ninja throwing stars.

Wow. We've been trying to bring the Nations together…and we ended up causing a food fight instead. And the weirdest part is that everyone's having a blast. It's like we almost managed to achieve the goal of Operation Happiness…in a twisted, food-fueled, *Hunger Games* kind of way.

But it's a start, right?

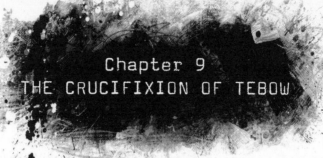

The next day, I wear an old pair of jeans and a sweatshirt to school, just in case anyone gets any more food-fight ideas during lunch. I go looking for Brainzilla and find the entire Freakshow gathered around Tebow's locker.

"Where did they get it?" Eggy asks.

"Wow, it really looks like you," Zitsy puts in. He touches the bloody nail in Jesus's hand. I mean no disrespect, but seriously, the statue is just, like, completely weird looking, like maybe it was made by one of those artists in prison you read about sometimes.

Help me, mortals!

Tebow is wearing the same look he had after the chili dog hit him in the head. I touch his shoulder. "I got the point with the chili dog," Tebow says.

"Well, look on the bright side," I tell him. "At least they don't think you're like Satan."

"If I were like Satan, they wouldn't mess with me," Tebow points out.

"Good call," Zitsy says. "Let's all be more like Satan, everybody."

"I call devouring souls!" Eggy shouts.

"Only if I can throw people into a lake of fire." Flatso points to the Freaky Jesus. "I'll start with whoever made this."

"Come on, you guys," I say, taking the Freaky Jesus and holding it up. "It's actually kind of cool. It can be our mascot."

"Let's dress it up for Halloween," Brainzilla suggests.

We switch to coming up with costume ideas for the statue. I'm for lab coat and Einstein wig, but Eggy is very adamant about going cowboy. Flatso says she can make it a little hat.

And just like that, we turned something weird and scary into something weird and funny.

Mostly.

"Lucky!" Flatso whispers when she sees my note. (She's no longer British in bio, by the way.)

"It's because I nearly flunked my lab," I tell her.

"Great idea!"

"What? No! I didn't do it on purpose!"

Flatso thinks this over, like she suspects I might be trying to get some one-on-one time with our cute teacher. Which I am not. "Hmm," she says.

Actually, I'm pretty embarrassed by my lab. I'm usually a great science student, but missing ten days a while back really put me behind. I don't want Winnie—Mr. Quinn…What am I supposed to call him? Anyway, I don't want him to think I'm an idiot.

"I'm not an idiot," I tell him after class.

"What? I didn't think you were." Winnie looks confused as students file out of the room. "The mistake you made is pretty common." He starts writing on my lab to show me what I did wrong, and all I can think is:

"You just missed a step," he tells me.

I snap out of my little reverie and realize I missed his entire explanation. He turns my paper—now full of his red marks— back around and smiles at me, and when I look into his eyes, I see that they're this really beautiful greeny-blue around the iris and sort of amber at the center. I'm so busy looking at his eyes, that when I reach for my paper, I accidentally touch his fingers. A jolt of electricity shoots through me, and I feel myself start to blush.

"Um, thanks," I mumble, and hurry out of the room so fast that I knock my shoulder against the doorframe and stumble into the hallway. Attractive!

"Hey!" Brainzilla grabs my arm and helps me stay upright. "You okay?"

I nod and mutter something, and then she thrusts a copy of *PlainSpeaking*—which is our student newspaper, of which she is the editor, of course—into my face. "Check it out! Hot off the press! Now look at the front page!"

"Winston Quinn is sixteen?" I ask.

"He's seventeen now," Brainzilla says. "Cool, right?"

Cool? Maybe. Maybe just weird. So I have this Downy-fresh crush on a cute teacher

Plain Speaking
NEW SCIENCE TEACHER GRADUATED MIT AT 16!
WINSTON QUINN:
"I've never been in high school before."
By Katie Sloane

THE MYSTERY OF MS. DONALDSON!

who's…my age? Does that make it better? Or worse? And how could I forget that Flatso is totally in love with him already?

I'm not sure. All I know is that now I'm having all kinds of Wrong Thoughts, and I don't know how to stop them.

Or even if I want to.

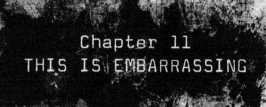

TGIF!

Totally Gonna Instantly Freak!

Just kidding. I mean, I know I've been in a mental hospital and my name is Cuckoo and all, but I actually think I'm pretty normal. You know, relatively.

And yet I *am* heading off to visit the school psychologist right now. Mr. Tool insists that I see Ms. Kellerman every Thursday at 2:30 PM.

"It's for your own good," Mr. Tool says. "Of course, we have to keep the best interests of all our students in mind."

Translation: *If Cuckoo goes nuts, I want someone to warn me that it's coming so I can keep the rest of the student body away from her and keep their parents from suing me.*

It really gives me the warm fuzzies to know how much he cares.

No, Warm Fuzzies! Not now! OFF! OFF! Go away!

Do not get me wrong: Ms. Kellerman isn't a bad person.

Mr. Tool, maybe, but Ms. Kellerman? No. It's just that she's a little *too* excited about handling my "case."

Ms. Kellerman is fine dealing with manic overachievers, recreational druggies, and girls who are considering having (but do not actually have) an eating disorder. But she's way out of her league when it comes to figuring me out. She's got a BA in psych while I spent ten days in a hospital with a bunch of MDs and PhDs, and only *one* of them ever really understood me.

Ms. Kellerman is also obsessed with my diary.

She's desperate to read it, but that is not happening. I won't let her set eyes on a single word. Not even a comma.

I usually spend my hour with her scribbling away, which really irks her. I'm not trying to be mean. It's just that the few times we've had a conversation, it hasn't really gone anywhere.

So I decided to stop talking. I prefer to just stay quiet and work on my new ending for each of the Twilight books. The series had a good ending, but like I said, I hate endings. Rewriting it gives me a way to make it seem less...permanent.

Hmm...let's see what else could happen: Zombie attack? Beach party? Ninja scene? Dance contest? Asteroid hitting Earth? "It was all a dream"?

None of those really grab me. So instead, I come up with a new ending for *The Hunger Games*, which feels easier—probably because I've only seen the movie and haven't read the book yet.

Oh, man. This is exactly why I can't show Ms. Kellerman my diary. I'm guessing she would have a full-blown field day with this.

I crack myself up.

Everybody's gonna die. Even you, Katniss and Peeta!

MAY THE ODDS BE EVER IN YOUR FAVOR

Berry juice

We were hungry.

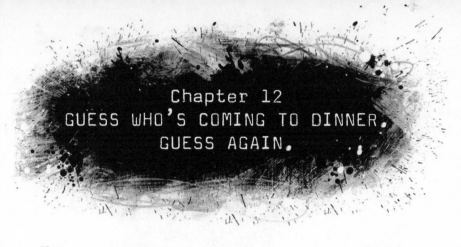

It's Thursday night, and Mrs. Morris is a little distracted. She's watching *Wheel of Fortune*, but she just doesn't seem into it. She usually guesses the phrases way before the contestants do—sometimes before a single letter has appeared on the board—but tonight she can't even figure out K__P O_ TRU_KI_G. Her mind is clearly elsewhere.

I'm pulling the ground beef out of the fridge and wondering what's up with her when I suddenly remember that tonight was the night Marjorie was supposed to come over, and I have a little Oprah-esque *aha!* moment.

Marjorie.

Is it fair that a complete cornflake like Marjorie got a sweet person like Mrs. Morris as a mother? I mean, is it? Even when Marjorie isn't here, she makes her mother miserable. And when she *is* here, it's worse.

I wish I could take Mrs. Morris's mind off her daughter. Just roll her out of here and meet up with some of my friends, maybe bomb around town. Let's see, who would be fun to hang out with? Laurence Darcy, of course. Probably not Holden

Caulfield, though. He's cool but not exactly fun. We'd want someone more like…Nicki Minaj, maybe?

I imagine us finding some nice restaurant. Parking right up front in the double-wide handicapped space, thanks to Mrs. Morris, then strolling up to the maître-d'. He'd take one look and give us a table right away.

There are only three flaws in this plan:

1. I have no car and no money.
2. I don't actually know Nicki Minaj.
3. Mrs. M would never recite Puff Daddy lyrics.

So, since we clearly aren't going to have dinner at an expensive restaurant with literary celebrities and rock stars, I decide to do the next best thing. I mix up some meat loaf and put it in the oven, then pull a tablecloth over the table and drag out the candlesticks. I get the wineglasses with the blue stems down from the top shelf and fill them with cranberry juice, which looks really pretty in the candlelight. By the time I call Mrs. Morris to the table, things are looking pretty festive.

Mrs. Morris gets into the spirit of our special meal by nearly chatting my ear off.

Okay, so she's not really a super-chatty person. But I can tell she appreciates the trouble I took by the way her eyes shine as she eats the meat loaf. Neither one of us mentions Marjorie.

After a while, I tell Mrs. Morris a little bit about Ms. Kellerman. Mrs. Morris listens carefully and clucks her tongue now and then sympathetically. She shakes her head, listening hard, and doesn't interrupt once, not even to say "really?" or "mmm." Most people have no idea how to listen that well.

When I've finished describing my "session," Mrs. Morris says, "Well, you were very patient with her, dear, and I think that's all anyone can ask."

Here's the thing: Mrs. Morris is made of awesome. She never tells me to put a smile on my face or goes on about how things were when she was my age. We're totally different, but she trusts me. And I trust her.

She *rolls* with my stuff.

No pun intended.

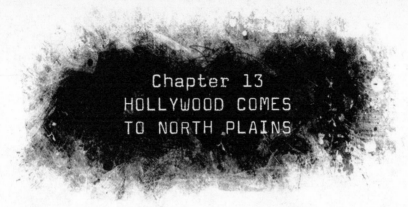

The minute I walk into school the next morning, I notice
something odd. It's quiet. Like, *library* quiet. But, weirdly,
the hallway is packed with students lingering by their lockers,
whispering to one another and giggling.

Mr. Tool is standing outside his office booming, "Good
morning!" to every student and teacher who wanders by.
Everyone ignores him. It's a truly peculiar vibe, and I can only
think of one explanation.

"Has the school been taken over by Pod People?" I ask Zitsy
when I run into him near my locker.

He laughs *way* too loudly, and I'm thinking, *Holy crap—the
Pods got him, too!* when Flatso jerks her head toward my Spanish
class with this wide-eyed look, like, *Clue in, dummy!* and that's
when I see this handsome older guy who looks a little like
Johnny Depp.

"Who's that?" I ask.

"Johnny Depp," Flatso says.

I look at the guy more carefully. "It doesn't look *exactly* like
Johnny Depp."

I stare at the handsome older guy a bit longer. He isn't

One of these things
is not like the others.

wearing a purple suit or crazy eyeliner, or anything. "How do you know it's him?"

Flatso gives me a look like I'm insane. "I know because I have a subscription to *Celeb Newz Weekly* and also because he's wearing a *name tag*."

Hmm. Aside from the fact that he's extremely handsome, this man could be anybody. He could just be a really, really, extremely, almost painfully good-looking substitute teacher, or a janitor, or something.

I'm actually a little weirded out by the thought that Johnny Depp is just a regular guy. I guess I don't want him to be. I want him to be the kind of artistic weirdo who never leaves home without an elaborate headdress and/ or eyeliner. I wonder if I should offer to lend him some, but he seems busy.

"What's he doing here?" I ask.

Flatso explains, "He's researching a role," at which point Zitsy hoots his Pod Person laugh again.

I turn to Zitsy. "Why are you laughing like that?"

"Is he looking over this way?" Zitsy's speaking without moving his lips.

I check. "No."

Mr. Depp is, in fact, still engrossed in the math book. But I realize that everyone around him is doing a very, very quiet version of going completely batshit.

Students and teachers are desperately trying to act cool yet somehow make Johnny Depp notice them. It's an interesting dynamic. The Thespians are singing in four-part harmony, as if they always hang out in the hallway doing that. The Twinkies are staring at Mr. Depp with flesh-melting intensity from behind their thick curtains of hair, so the effect is kind of lost. And the Goths seem to have added extra metal: on their necklaces, belts, wallets, ears, noses, lips, and eyebrows. Probably other places we don't need to mention, too.

For a moment, I think maybe I'll go over and say hello to Mr. Depp. He's a normal person, right? And so am I. I even have paperwork that says so.

But something holds me back. Even the thought of walking over to him makes me let out a creepy, nervous giggle.

It's weird, because a part of me thinks that Johnny Depp and I could really get along.

I wonder why he chose to come to North Plains High School instead of someplace closer to LA. Is it because we're more "normal" than LA kids? Maybe he's dying to meet normal people.

So part of me really believes that he'd like to talk to me, but another, bigger part of me doesn't dare say hello. He's an adult. And a celebrity. And I'm just…whoever I am. So even if he's dying to meet me but just doesn't know it, he isn't going to.

It's funny. He's here to observe us as normal high school students, but his being here has made everyone act bizarre. I have the strange feeling that Winnie Quinn was trying to tell us something about this the other day—that you can change something merely by observing it. Here it is, happening right before my eyes.

I love science.

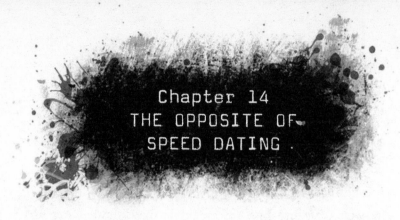

Chapter 14
THE OPPOSITE OF
SPEED DATING

What could possibly be weirder than having Johnny Depp come to your school?

You might want to sit down for this.

Tebow catches me right after school at my locker. The rest of the Freakshow is over near Eggy's corner, because she's handing out the Friday Candy. (Friday Candy was her idea. It's a fun way to celebrate the end of the week. It only happens once a month, though, and we never know which Friday it will be. Or what candy she'll bring.)

So Tebow catches me alone and asks me in this quiet voice if I want to go to a movie. I say sure, and then he scurries off without even getting any candy.

Wha???

I go over to the Freakshow to get their opinion, and when I explain the situation, they're like, "Wha???" too.

In the end, we decide that Tebow meant to ask just me, but nobody's really sure it's a date.

"Maybe he just wants to talk to you about something," Brainzilla says.

"Yeah," Zitsy agrees. "Like how much he wants to make out with you."

Flatso shoves Zitsy playfully, which sends him reeling halfway down the hall.

Eggy puts a hand on my shoulder. "Don't worry. It's just Tebow. He probably wants someone to see the latest action movie with. You'll have fun."

She's right. It's just Tebow.

So why do I suddenly feel completely sick and nervous?

Chapter 15
WHAT NOT TO WEAR

When I get home, I spend three hours trying to decide what to wear. If it's a date, I should look kind of nice. A skirt? But if it's not a date and I show up in a skirt, maybe Tebow will think that I thought it was a date. And then maybe things will get weird and awkward.

So then I think that maybe I should just wear what I already have on. But will that make Tebow think that I don't realize we're on a date?

I need help. Clearly. I start to dial Brainzilla, but I know that she'll want to come over with a bunch of different

Did you think this was a date? Because I didn't think it was, but now maybe I do. Or maybe I don't, and I have to find a way to make that clear without hurting your feelings.

Should I just put on some jeans?

outfit options. Flatso will want to give me a full makeover. Eggy will offer to lend me her *Cowboy Bebop* T-shirt. And Zitsy? I don't see any possibility of help there.

So I decide to do a mental check-in with my other BFFs— imagine what they might think.

Right. This is great advice…as long as it is translated into "wear something that Cuckoo would wear." Which is black cords, my softest green sweater, and a swipe of pale pink lipstick.

"Perfect," Laurence tells me. "You look neat and clean and elegant in a simple, understated way."

Nicki Minaj just shrugs, which I guess means that she's not impressed.

Tebow picks me up at exactly 7:13 PM. Mrs. Morris chirps out, "Have fun, sweetie!" as I climb into the front seat of Tebow's dad's very roomy Oldsmobile.

American cars of the 1980s: large and in charge.

And here is the weird thing—I'm sitting here with Tebow, who I see every day and frequently call on the phone at night, but *I can't think of anything to talk about*. I'm still obsessing over whether this is a date, which is complicated by the fact that I don't even know if I want this to be a date or not. Do I? Maybe. Tebow is insanely good looking. And sweet. But he's also Tebow. I've never thought of him that way, and I need a little time for my brain to try out the idea and see if I can get used to it.

That's when I notice that Tebow isn't talking, either. After a while, I decide I'm okay with quiet. And the minute I decide that, I remember something I wanted to tell him.

"Oh!" I pull my journal out of the messenger bag that I always carry around. "I made up a movie for us to star in."

(Don't worry—it's not the *Hunger Games* one.)

"You have a great imagination, Kooks," Tebow says. That makes me happy, even though I'm not really sure he gets my sense of humor. But it's okay. He doesn't have to get everything.

Eggy was right. It's just Tebow.

There's no need to overthink it.

THE MOVIE I CREATED FOR TEBOW
ENEMY PRISON CAMP
PRISON CAMP
BAD GUY'S MANSION
TEBOW'S MOVIE
CUCKOO CLARKE
CUT!
Will I lose my head????
THE KREMLIN
THE END
FILM RIGHTS AVAILABLE
CONTACT:
CUCKOO CLARKE
NORTH PLAINS, OREGON

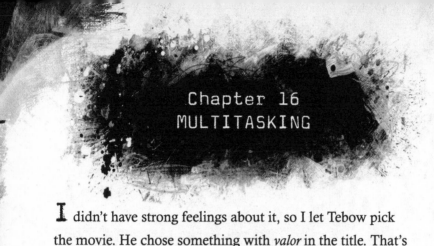

I didn't have strong feelings about it, so I let Tebow pick the movie. He chose something with *valor* in the title. That's Tebow's style. He likes soldier heroes who sacrifice all for friendship and/or country. He also likes inspirational true stories and action comedies. I like all that junk, too, so I was perfectly happy with *Valor Whatever*.

So we sat down and made fun of the commercial slideshow they were showing before the previews.

This feels good, because it's what we usually do with the Freakshow when we all see a movie. So there's less of the strange "I'm just out with Tebow for some reason" vibe.

Then the previews come on, and I remind Tebow that I'm going to punch him in the arm every time he tries to talk to me during the movie, same as I always do. The movie starts.

It's long and borderline incomprehensible, like maybe the script was cut and pasted from a lot of different movies and then jolted to life with a burst of lightning and a marketing committee.

On the other hand, there were a lot of great action scenes. And I really liked the characters. Maybe too much. Okay, I sobbed through the last ten minutes.

PEARL HARBOR
The Dirty Dozen
HART'S WAR
PLATOON
BLACK HAWK DOWN
SAVING PRIVATE RYAN

It's alive!

Is it?

IT'S A MONSTER MASH-UP!

Here are the highlights:

1. There were soldiers in the movie.
2. Tebow's fingers touched mine when we both reached for popcorn at the same time.
3. There was something gross on the floor right in front of my seat, and no matter where I moved my foot, my shoe kept getting stuck in it.
4. I was reasonably sure I could've written a better movie.

I even came up with several excellent alternate scenes and endings as it was going on.

After the movie, we walk around the mall for a while and get cappuccinos. I keep thinking, "This seems like a date. Not really. Well, maybe," and on and on like that.

Then Tebow drives me home, and I never really get up the nerve to ask if this was a friends deal or a date deal. And he doesn't bring it up, either.

So it just hangs there like a stinky fish that everyone's too afraid to touch while we say good night.

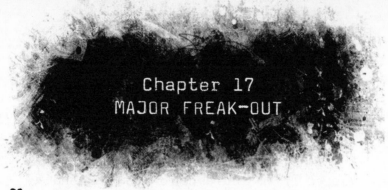

"Mrs. Morris?" I call as I step into the living room. I hear Tebow's car pull away as the door clicks closed behind me.

The talking heads on the evening news are blabbing, sending blue-and-white light flickering across the walls. Mrs. Morris is usually sitting right there—right in front of the television—from 10:00 to 11:00 PM. Cold snakes writhe through my stomach.

"Mrs. Morris?" I call. "Mrs. Morris?" I try to keep the rising panic out of my voice. Where is she? My skin feels cold and shuddery, like I've stepped into a giant spiderweb.

The clatter of toenails, then Morris the Dog bursts into the living room, barking hysterically. God, if only this were an episode of *Lassie*!

What is it, Morris? What? She's trapped in a well down by the old mill? Let's go!

WOOF WOOF

"What? What is it?" I ask, and I am so temporarily insane that (a) my first idea is that Mrs. Morris has been *kidnapped* and (b) I don't even notice that the back door is open until Morris practically drags me toward it.

That's when I hear "Yoo-hoo!" coming from the garage, and when I burst in, I find Mrs. Morris sprawled across the floor.

"Oh my god!" I'm crying and halfway hysterical—it's like that *Bridesmaids* moment all over again—but Mrs. Morris is all cheerful and acting like it's perfectly normal that she has fallen out of her wheelchair and is lying splayed across a slab of concrete.

"I didn't mean to worry you, dear," she says gently. "I just wanted some paper towels, and they were a little out of my reach, so I took a spill."

Oh, don't mind me, dear. How was your evening with that nice boy?

She reaches for my hand, and we sit there for a moment, our fingers interlaced. Her gray hair is pooled around her head on the concrete. I keep trying to say, "You didn't worry me," but my throat is clogged, and I can't speak at all. All I can do is make a wheezy-squeaky noise, which sets the wrinkles in Mrs. Morris's face to worry mode.

"Oh dear," she says. "Oh dear. Oh, oh, I'm so sorry."

I take a deep, shaky breath and wipe the snot that's pouring from my nose all over my sleeve.

"It's all right. I'm all right, dear." Mrs. Morris's voice is a gentle whisper, and I realize that she's trying to calm me down. I take another breath, forcing myself to pull it together. I sit there with my eyes closed until my tears dry up. When I open them, Mrs. Morris's dark eyes are watching me.

"I'm okay," I tell her. "I'm okay, too. I didn't mean to worry you, either. I'm sorry."

"No, *I'm* sorry."

"No, really, *I'm* sorry," I insist, and then I realize how ridiculous that sounds, and I let out a shallow little snort-chuckle. Then Mrs. Morris giggles. And after a minute, the whole thing starts to seem really funny, and soon neither of us can stop laughing.

After a while, our laughter quiets down. Then I lock my arms around her and haul her into her wheelchair. Luckily, Mrs. Morris only weighs about ninety pounds.

Nothing broken. No harm done.

Except for the major flashbacks I'm having to when my mom skipped out.

I'm still shaking like I may never stop.

Chapter 18
HERE IS WHAT HAPPENED

People always want to know what happened.

The answers are: no, no, not more than most people, and yes.

Look, my mom isn't a horrible person. She's just kind of flaky. Which is great if you're piecrust, but not so great when you're responsible for the welfare of another human being.

My mom goes through boyfriends faster than I go through a box of Kleenex during a *Bridesmaids* marathon. Whenever she starts a new fling, she disappears for a few days. That has been happening since I was seven or eight.

The thing is, my grandmother used to live across the street from us. So when Mom would disappear, I'd just head over there. Mom usually came back after a day or two. The longest she was ever away was five nights.

But Grammy died two years ago. And this time, Mom has been gone for two months, eleven days, and fifteen hours.

For the first two days, I hardly even worried. I just ate peanut-butter sandwiches and made sure I got to school on time. But after a week, I was low on food. Mom hadn't left me any money.

After two weeks, I started bursting into tears at the slightest problem.

After a month, my hair started to fall out in clumps. I lost eight pounds. I was flunking math.

Finally, after my *Bridesmaids* meltdown, the Freakshow staged an intervention and demanded to know what was going on. I didn't want to get Mom in trouble, but I didn't know what to do, so I told them.

Naturally, Brainzilla was on the case right away. She called Child Protective Services and got in touch with Mrs. Morris, my neighbor. Mrs. Morris said that of course I could come and stay with her, but the state wanted me to have an "observation period" before they released me into her custody. So I got down at Crazytown.

And that's how I ended up in this life.

Poor Mrs. Morris. I know she feels bad that she scared me out there in the garage. It isn't her fault, of course. It isn't my fault, either.

There's no one to blame. No one who's around, anyway.

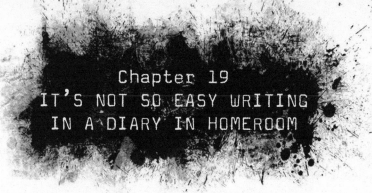

Homeroom is nothing but dead air this morning. I don't feel much like writing. Still no luck with the new ending for Twilight. For a while, I was working on a musical number. But I can't write music. And it's hard to get the dance steps across in a book.

Uh-oh I think they've gone BATTY!

Yeah...but it's the first time I've seen them smile.

So that's not working.

Half the class is zoning out, and the other half is trying to carve expletives onto the desks, so nobody notices as I take a little mental vacay and go visit Laurence.

The English countryside is way more beautiful this morning than dreary suburban Portland. (No offense, suburbs!)

So I'm sitting there, mentally running through a field of flowers, when it's like a heavy weight lands on me. You know what's worse than having a football lineman pull you out of a back-row seat? It's some football lineman sitting on you because he didn't even notice you were there.

I try to gasp but can't get enough
oxygen. Tommy Marinachi has got to
weigh two-eighty.

Interestingly, it's Marty Bloom
who notices I need help. "Jeez, Marinachi!"
he says, smacking Tommy on the side of the
head and hauling him off me.

Tommy apologizes as I try to massage
some feeling back into my legs. "I'm so sorry! I didn't even see
you!"

He's only making me feel worse. "I'm okay."

Marty looks doubtful. "Are you sure?" he asks. "Do you
want me to carry you to the nurse or something?"

"No, really," I say. "I can feel the blood returning to this one
already." I attempt to move my foot, and fail. Any minute now.

Marty looks concerned, but he doesn't push it. I'm grateful. I
mean, I haven't even spoken to him since that whole food fight/
Freaky Jesus deal.

It would definitely be a little weird to have him carry me to
the nurse.

I just wish I could figure Bloom out.

Nice?

Mean?

Why can't he just be one thing or the other?

Chapter 20
THE FREAKSHOW'S OPERATION HAPPINESS: HOLIDAY EDITION

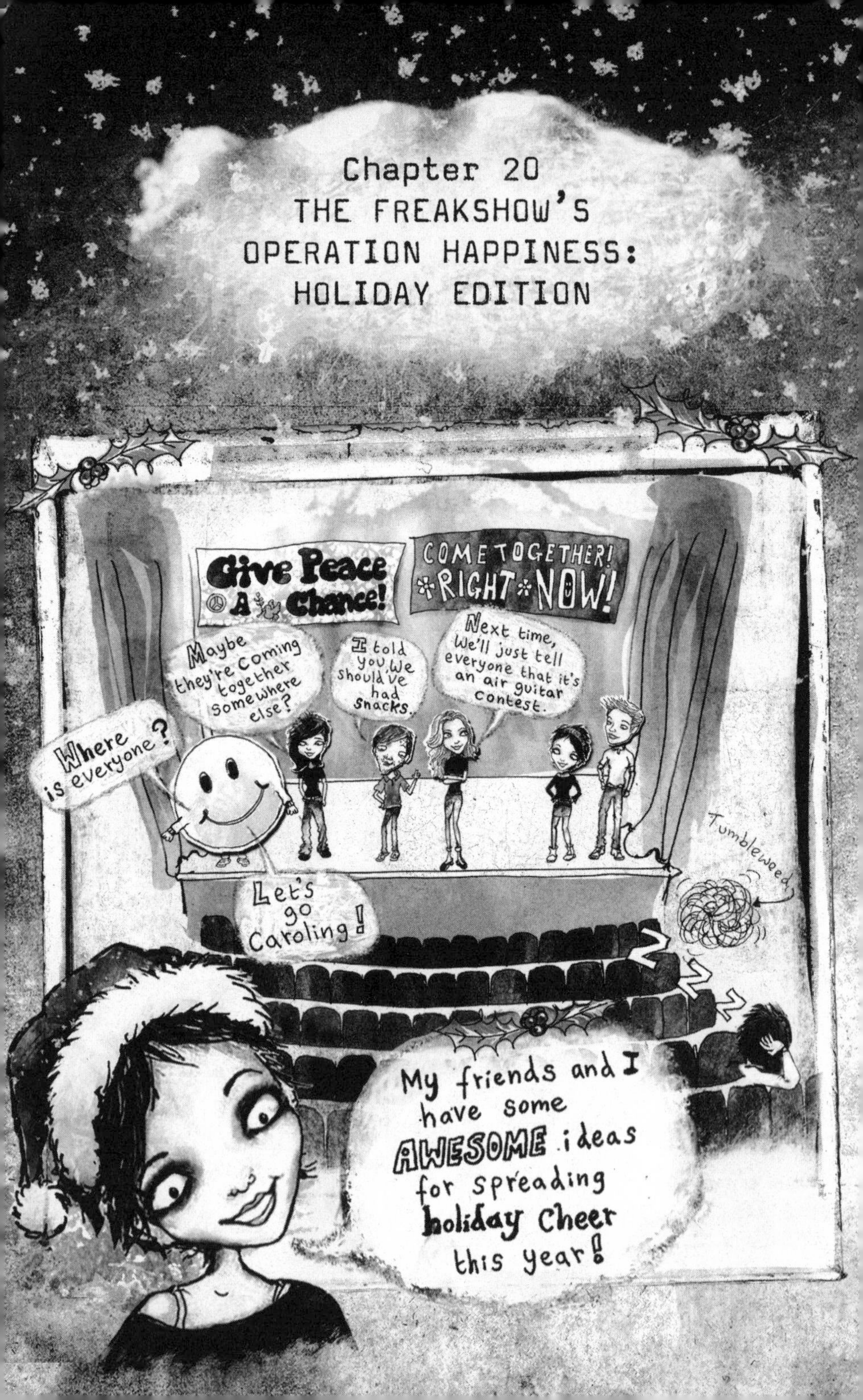
Give Peace A Chance!
COME TOGETHER! RIGHT NOW!
Where is everyone?
Maybe they're coming together somewhere else?
I told you, we should've had snacks.
Next time, we'll just tell everyone that it's an air guitar contest.
Let's go Caroling!
Tumbleweed
ZZZ
My friends and I have some AWESOME ideas for spreading holiday cheer this year!

Joy
I haven't been that good, but you'll still bring me some good stuff, right?
I can't feel my lap!
Why are those grown-ups bothering Santa?
Wait! You didn't get my good side!
Say "Rudolph"!
to the WORLD

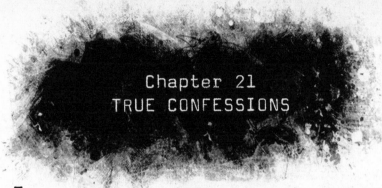

Chapter 21
TRUE CONFESSIONS

I love taking the bus to Portland. It's fun to watch people whiz past the windows as I ride along, imagining their lives. There are worse ways to spend a sleety Saturday.

The bus is so toasty that I have to take off my coat, which is fine with me. Mrs. Morris insists that the cold air is good for her circulation, so she keeps our place pretty chilly. The bus is a nice change from my seven-degree bedroom.

It's already mid-December, and everyone around me is loaded down with red and silver shopping bags. I'm not going shopping, though. I'm actually on my way to see Dr. Marcuse. She's the one from Crazytown and she is 100 percent awesome with zero byproducts. I'm serious.

Anyway, don't worry—nothing dramatic has happened. Well, nothing except this mild freak-out I had the other day when I tried to borrow Brainzilla's turtleneck.

Once I got the turtleneck off my head and took a few deep breaths, I realized that Katie was right. Not just because of the turtleneck, but also because of how worried I got when I couldn't find Mrs. Morris the other night. And also because I really like Dr. Marcuse.

Not because I'm having a psychiatric emergency. I swear.

Anyway, I make it to St. Augustine, and I just have to ask, is it weird to say that a mental hospital feels homey?

I actually feel kind of happy to be back here. It's a bit like visiting my old elementary school: There's my old locker! There's my old teacher! There's that same dead fly that has been on the windowsill for three months!

But it's also like visiting your old school in that there are all these new faces. I check in at the desk, then walk past the cozy activity room where a bunch of teen girls are using safety scissors to cut up magazines for a collage. Right. It's Saturday— art therapy. Mr. Noyes is smiling at one of the girls, explaining something in his slow, patient way, gesturing with his tiny, clean hands. He doesn't notice me as I pause in the doorway, remembering what it was like to be one of those girls at the white table.

I don't feel any crazier now than I did then.

Laughter bubbles from the activity room as I move toward Dr. Marcuse's office. Light streams in through the large windows, lighting up the colorful fish mural that lines the hall. A nurse in Tweety Bird scrubs pushes a medication cart out of one of the rooms. Her face lights up with a huge smile.

"Hey, there, Ms. Maggie," Opal says, waving at me with her fabulous nails. They're painted with little Tweety Birds. "Guess you missed us too much?"

"I'm just here to check in with Dr. Marcuse," I say, walking into her soft-bodied hug. She smells like hand cream.

"Well, you're looking real good, sweetheart. You take care of yourself." And Opal gives me a little squeeze, like she really is happy to see me, and really is happy I'm better.

Here is the thing about Crazytown: It's shockingly normal. It isn't like the mental hospitals you see in movies, where the staff is all psycho and desperate to give people lobotomies. Even

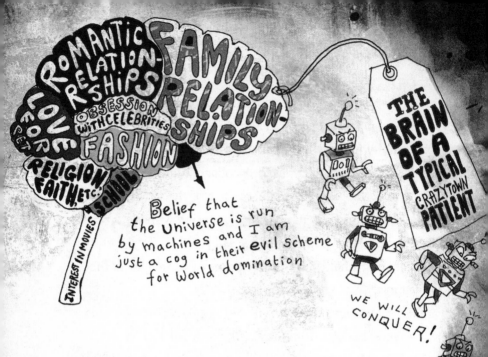

ROMANTIC RELATION-SHIPS

LOVE FOR PET

OBSESSION WITH CELEBRITIES

FASHION

FAMILY RELATIONSHIPS

RELIGION FAITH, ETC.

INTEREST IN MOVIES

SCHOOL

Belief that the Universe is run by machines and I am just a cog in their evil scheme for World domination

THE BRAIN OF A TYPICAL CRAZYTOWN PATIENT

WE WILL CONQUER!

the so-called patients wouldn't strike you as nutcases. That's because most of the crazy goes on inside their heads.

At Crazytown, the staff encourages you to, like, live in the real world most of the time. Then, with your doctor, you work on those little parts of your brain that are tripping you up. So most of the day is spent doing art or playing games or exercising or whatever. It's kind of like camp. Minus the archery.

Dr. Marcuse's door is half open, like it's inviting me in, but I give a soft knock anyway.

"Maggie, is that you?" she calls, and when I walk in, she gets up from behind her desk and comes over to grab my hands. Dr. Marcuse isn't a very huggy person, but I can tell she likes me.

I sit down in the same old comfortable wing chair. When

I was at Crazytown, I saw Dr. Marcuse every day, sometimes twice a day. I know every detail of this room: the slightly crooked diploma from Columbia on the wall behind her head, the elegant aloe plant on her dark wood desk, the framed print of a yellow elephant that sits propped among the books on her disordered shelves, the green fabric wall hanging.

Who wouldn't get better in a place like this, talking to someone like Dr. Marcuse? After ten days, she pronounced me "sound of mind." I'm totally fine now. Mostly totally fine. Still a little blue sometimes, but hey—it worked for Picasso, right?

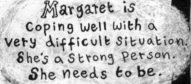

Chapter 22
INDEPENDENT

There's a great indie bookstore about five blocks from my house called Pagemakers, where I like to spend some of my time and most of my money. It always has a great selection of books, and sometimes it hosts readings by awesome authors. Usually only, like, three people show up to the readings, so I always get to ask lots of questions and get my book signed, and it's really great. But this evening, the store's hosting one of my favorite authors, Nancy Werlin, and her fans are hogging up some serious floor space. It's also mid-December, so the place is buzzing with holiday shoppers.

I take a seat near the back of the room. There's a guy in a baseball hat sitting in front of me, and its flipped-up brim is blocking my view, so I lean forward and tap him on the shoulder.

"Excuse me," I say politely. "Would you mind taking off your hat? I can't see the podium."

The guy turns and looks at me. He's handsome, about my age, with pink cheeks and eyes like a crisp sky. "Sure, Cuckoo," he says with a smile.

Have you ever seen one of those pictures that look like a candlestick until you look at it a different way and realize it's, like, two friends talking to each other? Sometimes the new picture comes to you suddenly. Like, you didn't see it and didn't see it, and then—suddenly—it's there.

That's what happens to this guy's face as he takes off his baseball cap. Suddenly, this super-cute dude in front of me morphs into Winnie Quinn, my biology teacher.

"Oh!" I say. "Hi, Mr. Quinn."

He looks vaguely horrified by the use of his Teacher name.

"I mean, um, Winnie," I add awkwardly. I hurry to change the subject. "Are you a fan?"

Winnie holds up three books. "I get this one autographed every time she comes to town." He opens the cover of *Rules of Survival* and shows me the title page. *Nancy Werlin* is signed in five places.

I pull open my copy of *Double Helix*.

"Wow," Winnie breathes when he sees my seventeen Nancy Werlin signatures.

"Which is your favorite?" I ask.

"*Impossible*," Winnie says as pink sweeps up his cheeks. "I know it's not the most macho choice," he rushes on, "but I read it a bunch of times when I was in college and I couldn't go out with everyone else because I wasn't old enough to get into the bars and it just kind of spoke to me and…uh…sorry. I'm babbling. I should've just said *Rules of Survival*."

"I love both of those books," I tell him honestly. "I can't wait to read her new one."

I realize I'm fidgeting wildly with the cover of my book, flipping it back and forth between my hands. Why am I so on edge? He must think I'm a nut job, which I am certifiably *not* (now). But it's just so weird to see him outside the classroom and talk to him like we're two regular teenagers hanging out at a book signing. (Except *regular* teenagers, sadly, don't usually go to book signings.)

"Me neither." The dimple in Winnie's right cheek winks at me, and I'm tempted to reach out and touch it lightly with my finger, but just then, Ms. Jackson, the owner of Pagemakers, steps to the front of the room, and everyone gets quiet. Ms. Werlin stands to the side, smiling brilliantly as the toad-voiced Ms. Jackson gives her introduction, and Winnie turns around in his seat.

For the next hour, I try to concentrate on Ms. Werlin's words and the section of her latest novel that she shares with us. But all I can think about is the handsome boy in front of me, my biology teacher, the teenager who never got to go to high school, the college student who probably spent his nights alone.

I can't help wondering what things would be like if he were a student instead of a teacher. Would we be friends?

I don't see how we could help it.

The thought makes me just a little bit sad.

You know that feeling when you wake up and you're all cozy
in bed and then you remember, *It's Christmas!*

Well...

It's Christmas!

The minute my eyes snap open, I fling off my covers,
which is a huge mistake because it's freezing in my room.
Luckily, Brainzilla gave me a Snuggie as an early holiday
present yesterday. I slip it on and yank a pair of socks over
the pair I had on in bed. Then I hurry downstairs—although
I'm not really sure why. I mean, Mrs. Morris made me
promise not to get her a gift, and I can't imagine that she's
gotten me one.

The other day, Winnie Quinn told us about Pavlov and his
dog. Pavlov would ring a bell, then give the dog a treat. After
a while, the dog would drool whenever it heard a bell—even
without the treat. Christmas is kind of like that, I guess. Glee is
hardwired into our brains.

Even for people who don't believe in Santa, there's
something magical about Christmas morning. Our tiny fake
tree covered in tiny white lights looks surprisingly elegant in
the pale winter morning light. And someone has put a few

gifts in my stocking: a candy cane and a battered copy of *The Complete Poems of Emily Dickinson.*

I run my fingers over the faded gold letters on the cloth cover. When I open it, the book lets off a sweet, old-book smell. Mrs. Morris has written me a message in her shaky handwriting.

There are some gifts that are so perfect that you can never, ever express how much they mean to you.

Dear Maggie,
Merry Christmas!
I'm so glad we can share this home.
Yours,
Mrs Morris

OEMS OF

kinson

I hear someone banging in the kitchen and go in to find Mrs. Morris pulling something from the oven. "Good morning!" she says when she sees me. "Merry Christmas!"

I rush to help her with the hot pan. It's full of warm, gooey sticky buns. "Oh, Mrs. Morris," I say, "I thought we weren't doing presents!" I feel bad that she's gone to all this trouble.

"Now, sweetheart, you should know that being able to fuss over you is a present to me," Mrs. Morris says. "I haven't made sticky buns in years. No reason to."

"Well...I do have a present for you," I say.

Mrs. Morris clucks and frowns. "I told you not to buy me anything."

"I didn't buy it. I made it." I hurry upstairs and return with a scroll.

Mrs. Morris smiles when she unrolls it. "Well, isn't that sweet. A family portrait!"

It's a picture I drew of the two of us and Morris the Dog. I had considered adding Nicki Minaj and Laurence, too, but wasn't sure that Mrs. Morris would realize I was joking.

Mrs. Morris gives me a hug. "This is one of the nicest gifts I've ever received," she says, and dabs at her eyes a little with an oven mitt. She puts the picture on the fridge while I give Morris the Dog his special Christmas treat—a large green dog biscuit. I pull out a chair for Mrs. Morris, then serve us each a sticky bun on a plate along with some coffee. (Mine is mostly milk with four tablespoons of sugar.)

After we clean up from breakfast, we go into the living room to watch *Elf*.

It's not the most exciting, expensive holiday...but it feels warm and cozy. As I sit on the couch beside Mrs. Morris, I realize I'm happier than I have been in a long time.

I guess making the sticky buns wore Mrs. Morris out a little, because she falls asleep near the end of the movie. I hold her delicate, papery hand for a while.

I'm filled with gratitude for her, and I remind myself not to take her for granted. I've been so wrapped up in my own life that I haven't been thinking about her nearly enough. But, really, where would I be without Mrs. Morris?

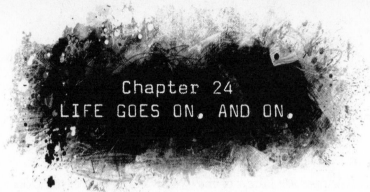

Chapter 24
LIFE GOES ON. AND ON.

Call me sentimental, but I think the holiday season is really all about one thing: money.

Big bucks. Crazy cash.

Well, that's what it seems to be about at the country club. I've been working tons of parties this holiday week and raking in the dough.

I don't mind the work, to be honest with you. Even servitude has its moments. Brainzilla and I agreed to work both the Christmas and New Year's gigs. Eggy joins us for a few of the midweek parties. She doesn't really need the money, but the club is desperate for extra help, and she finds the place pretty humorous.

Excuse me, miss, but I think the milk in this cappuccino is two percent instead of the skim I asked for.

Ha! Good one!

During the New Year's party, Brainzilla is everywhere—hostessing, busing, smoothing linens, soothing egos. She never has enough money and always has a million jobs, and the amazing thing is that she's good at everything. Who's that Indian goddess? The one with all the arms? Shakti—that's Brainzilla.

Pat Pat

After three straight days of parties, all the country club members start to look alike to me. I have this fantasy that everyone at the club has the same mother. They must at least be cousins, right? What's the probability of there being that many people with great skin in the same room? It *has* to be genetics.

aaa

I'm everyone's mother here at the club, but let's keep that to ourselves. Mum's the word. Ha-ha! I find puns so terribly droll, don't you, darling?

"May I have this dance?" Marty Bloom catches my elbow gently and stops me at the edge of the dance floor. It takes me a moment to recognize him. He's wearing a tuxedo with the bow tie dangling loose, and he looks very James Bond-y and dangerously handsome.

I nod at the tray in my hands. "I'm working."

"Just one dance."

"No, really, I can't—" But he has taken my tray and placed it on the bar. "Okay, I need that back—" Ignoring my words, he takes my hand and leads me to the dance floor. It feels strange to be touching Bloom. His hand is warm and large, and I spend a lot of time worrying that mine is small and sweaty, and wishing that someone made hand antiperspirant.

The band is playing some sort of slow swing thing. Marty wraps his arms around my waist, which means that I have no choice but to wrap my arms around his neck, which makes me feel a little dizzy and awkward. I'm so close to Bloom that I can smell the cinnamon scent of his breath. Mints? Gum? He smells delicious.

I catch Eggy scowling at me from the edge of the dance floor. *What are you doing?* she mouths.

I shrug, and a little shiver runs through me. Bloom is tall, and I'm enjoying standing next to him. He rests his chin on my head, and I feel strangely safe.

And just as I'm enjoying that feeling, someone taps me on the shoulder.

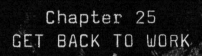

Where's my caviar, damn it?

Excuse me, Ms. Clarke." The hard brown eyes of my manager—Mr. Wong—are boring into my skull. "You're supposed to be working, not dancing."

"Oh, sorry—I just…" I pull away from Bloom, but he takes my hand again.

"Excuse me," Bloom says, flashing a brilliant smile. "I've asked Ms. Clarke to dance with me. You don't mind—do you?"

"Actually, I do." Mr. Wong folds his arms across his chest. "People are waiting for their orders."

Bloom scans the room, as if he's only just noticed the tables. "Oh, I'm sure these people can wait. I know my father—right over there—can." He waves at his father, who grins and waves back.

Mr. Wong's face goes pale. "Oh, you're Albert Bloom's son?"

"That's right," Bloom says.

Mr. Wong's eyes dart from Bloom to me to Mr. Bloom. "Oh,

well—" Mr. Wong straightens his tie. "Well, Ms. Clarke, I don't think a little dance will hurt anyone. Go ahead, go ahead. Ha, ha! You kids have fun!" He claps Bloom on the back, and I watch him scurry away.

"Wow," I say. "Cool."

Bloom's shoulder rises, then dips. "Everyone's afraid of my dad."

"That sounds awesome."

"It's not that awesome," Marty says, and a strange look flashes across his face, which disappears as quickly as it came. "But it is useful sometimes. So, Maggie—let me ask you something." Marty lifts my arm, and I twirl.

"Why do you spend so much time with Tebow and those other guys?" Marty asks.

I feel suddenly wary, as if Marty is trying to catch me in a trap. "Well—they're kind to me," I say carefully. "They get me. And I know I can count on them when I need it."

Marty looks thoughtful. "But they're so weird."

"Everyone is," I reply, "once you get to know them."

"Interesting," he says, and— *bam!*—I feel like I've totally scored one for Operation Happiness.

Okay, just don't drop me.

Meh-
Jury's
Still out.

I dance with Marty until the band strikes up a new song, at which point my manager looks like he's about to bust a vein in his forehead, so I excuse myself and dash off to fill more drink orders.

"What was that?" Eggy demands while I'm waiting at the bar.

Out of nowhere, Brainzilla appears at my shoulder. "Why were you dancing with a Hater?"

"He's not as bad as you guys think," I say.

"He's worse," Eggy snaps.

"I thought we weren't going to be so judgmental," I remind her.

"That doesn't mean that we're tossing all our judgment out the window," Brainzilla shoots back.

I wonder. Can people change?

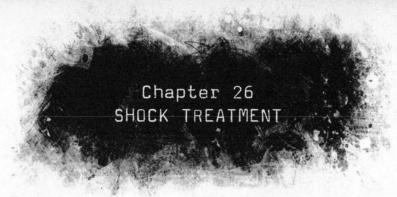

"Don't go," Brainzilla says.

Marty just offered me a ride home. Eggy's shift ended two hours ago and mine just ticked "done," and I'm ready to drop. As a shift lead, Brainzilla still has to finish counting receipts, which could take another hour.

"I'll be done in twenty minutes," Brainzilla promises. "You know I'm fast. And Mom is already on the way."

"If I wait here, I'll probably fall asleep at the bar," I say. "I'm telling you, Marty is an Operation Happiness waiting to happen."

I wipe down the counter and then yank off my apron. My feet feel like concrete blocks at the ends of my legs.

It's nice to see that someone around here knows how to observe proper manners. Unlike the woman currently vomiting white wine into the ladies' room toilet.

I wish someone would go ahead and invent that beaming-up technology they have on *Star Trek*. Forget the Internet—I want to get beamed straight to bed.

"All right, all right," Brainzilla says. "See you tomorrow."

I lean over the counter to give my bestie a peck on the cheek, then head toward the coatroom, where Marty is already waiting for me. He's actually holding my coat when I arrive, and I'm just about ready to promote the guy to Bona Fide Human Being.

Marty holds the door for me as we step outside, and he escorts me to his beautiful car, waiting as I slip into the comfortable seat. He closes the door, shutting me inside the dark cocoon. Wow. Plush leather. And it's so clean on the inside. My mom's car was always approximately 80 percent candy bar wrappers.

Marty settles into his seat and looks over at me. I smile at him. "Thanks for the ride" is about to spill from my lips—when he grabs my wrist and lays his mouth on mine. I try to speak, but his lips stop my voice, his boozy breath stinking up my nostrils. He must have spent the past three hours with a bottle of gin, because his cinnamon scent has disappeared.

I push against him, but his grip tightens. He's smothering me, crushing me. Adrenaline courses through me, but the more I fight to get away, the stronger he seems, and fear starts to choke me.

I try to scream, and Marty shoves his hand over my mouth as his other hand reaches up my skirt. The fear really starts to get me, and I think, *I'll never get him off. I'm not strong enough—I can't fight him*, and just at that moment, I remember something that Flatso told me: "The jaw is the strongest muscle in the body."

So I bite down on his hand.

Hard.

Bloom bleeds all over the place, and I spill out of the car and onto the freezing asphalt.

"Kooks?" Brainzilla is there—she hauls me to my feet, takes one look at Marty, screaming and bleeding in his car and slams the door, silencing him.

"Oh my god." I pull her into a hug, but she's already moving, half hugging me, half dragging me across the parking lot. She says, "It's okay—Mom is here. I told you I'm fast. It's okay. It's all okay," and in another moment, we're standing in the headlights of Brainzilla's mom's 1998 Corolla. I have never been so happy to see a midsize sedan in my life.

"What's wrong?" Brainzilla's mom asks as we climb into the backseat, but my best friend just shakes her head and says, "Please drive, Mom, okay?" Mrs. Sloane does, and she doesn't ask questions. Brainzilla and her mom are close, so she doesn't need to ask questions. She knows she'll get the whole story later.

I lean against my best friend, and something tickles my face. I swipe at it and realize it's drying blood. Bloom's blood. I nearly barf, but Katie just pulls me close, and I can smell her familiar smell of coconut shampoo and vanilla body spray— like a macaroon—and I feel a bit better. And she doesn't say anything like "I told you so" or "See? Bloom's bad news" as her mom drives home. She just holds my hand as I cry.

It's only two hours into the new year, and already things are not looking good.

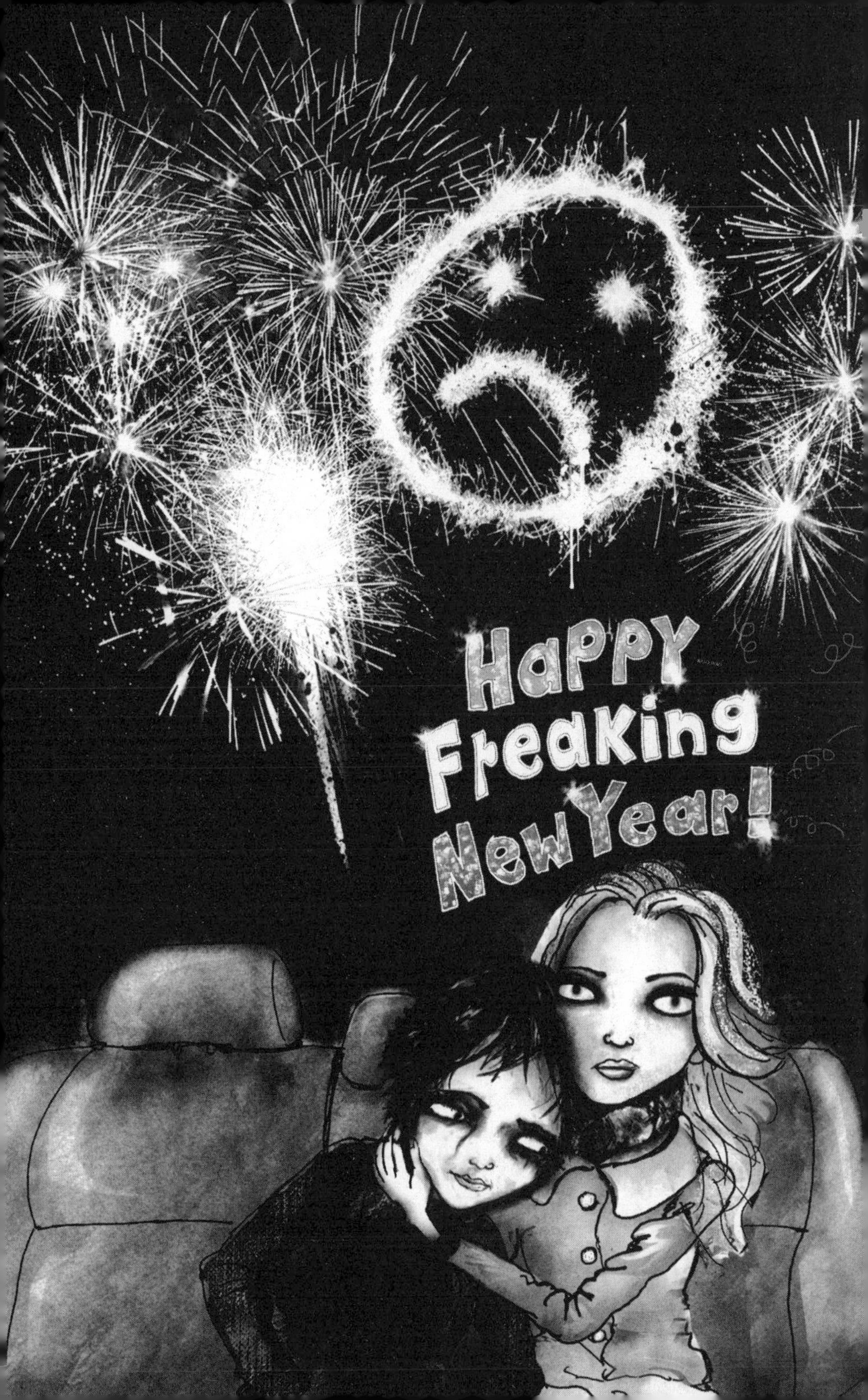
Happy
Freaking
New Year!

I want to go home with Katie, but it's too late to call Mrs. Morris, and if I'm not there in the morning, she'll probably call 911 and mount a posse to look for me.

So Brainzilla's mom drops me off at home. I manage to thank her for the ride in a somewhat normal voice and walk up the front steps.

The moment I hear Mrs. Sloane drive away, this clammy feeling comes over me. It drips from my head, down my neck, all over my body. It's a clinging ick.

It captures me; I can't go inside.

I'm not someone who gets feelings. I usually just walk right into stuff. But this time, it's like there's a force field around the house.

I hear the television blaring in the living room. It's a familiar, calming sound. Then I realize something. It's 3:17 AM. Mrs. Morris is usually asleep by eleven.

Why is the TV on?

Fear hooks into me, painful enough to pull me forward.

She fell down again, I tell myself. *She just fell down again, shefelldownagain, SHEFELLDOWNAGAIN,* SHEJUSTFELLDOWNAGAIN! My brain is screaming, wailing like an alarm as I fall to my knees beside Mrs. Morris.

She doesn't wake up when I say her name. I touch her wrist—it's cold…and I can't find a pulse.

"Katie!" I scream, and crawl on my knees to the front door, but my best friend and her mother have already driven away. Still, I scream again. "Katie!" echoes down the deserted street.

This isn't happening, I think as I crawl back toward Mrs. Morris. *I'm dreaming.* But I know I'm not. My black tights catch on a flooring nail and rip down the shin. The nail scrapes my skin, drawing blood, but I barely feel it.

Morris the Dog is licking Mrs. Morris's face, and when I start to cry, he comes and licks my tears instead. I didn't know tears could pour from me so hard and fast. They say that the human body can be as much as 75 percent water, and I feel like it all comes spewing from my eyes and mouth and nose at once. My body just convulses with the weight of that water as I run my fingers over Mrs. Morris's face and through her hair. I even spill a little drool on her cheek and have to wipe it away with my coat sleeve.

I crawl to the phone and dial 911, and the operator can hardly understand a word I'm saying. It doesn't matter, though; 911 magic means she knows where I'm calling from, and I'm so hysterical that she says she'll send an ambulance right away. "You have to breathe, miss," she says over and over, but I can't breathe. I feel like someone is sitting on me.

Finally, I manage a raggedy inhale. Then another.

The 911 operator keeps talking softly into my ear, telling me that help is coming and to try to stay calm, but I'm not really listening to her. I sit down to think. It takes me a few minutes to realize that I'm sitting in Mrs. Morris's wheelchair.

Chapter 28
I STILL DON'T WAKE UP

I sit in the wheelchair and breathe deeply. That's when I notice that Mrs. Morris's eyes are still open—and they're looking at me.

Those dead eyes completely unnerve me. They look like Mrs. Morris's eyes, but with none of their warmth and energy—no sparkle. I lean forward and try to close them, but it's not as easy as it looks in the movies—her eyelids spring open again, which makes me let out a little scream. I jump back into the wheelchair, completely freaked.

How long will it take for the ambulance to get here? I wonder. Well, however long it is—that's too long. The operator is still talking, asking me questions that I don't even realize I'm murmuring answers to. But I can't hang out with Mrs. Morris's dead eyes on me, and I'm not going to just go up to my room and rearrange my bookshelf, either. It isn't easy to just sit in a room with someone you love who's now dead.

And before I know what I'm doing, I've tossed the phone on to the couch and rolled right through the front door and down the ramp. I don't even pause to get out of the wheelchair— that's how freaked out I am.

The air is cold on my face as I wheel down the street. It's the first day of January, but we haven't had much snow, so the sidewalks are clear as I race beneath the bare trees. My face stings, and I realize that it's because my tears are starting to freeze.

A few lights come on, but I keep going.

I circle the block, and by the time I get back, the blue and red ambulance lights are flickering against the front of our house. A police car is there, too.

I roll up the ramp in the wheelchair, and a tall police officer with a big nose tries to stop me. "Sorry, miss," he says. "There's been an accident."

"I know," I explain. "I'm the one who called 911."

The officer is really nice then. I follow him into the kitchen while the paramedics take care of Mrs. Morris. Of course, I have to answer a lot of questions. I'm a little muddy brained, but I answer as well as I can. I have to take a lot of breaks, though. I can't quite catch my breath.

Finally, the short officer says, "You'll have to come with us to the hospital. There's a lot of paperwork, I'm afraid."

"Okay," I say, standing up.

I don't think they were expecting that.

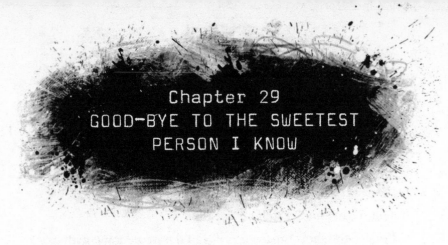

I stay with Eggy for a couple of days.

Her parents are very sweet to me, but they're shy. Which is fine. All I want is to be alone.

Eggy is a great friend. She knows how to be quiet, and she is always ready to download ridiculous movies and episodes of bad reality television. We spend a lot of time eating ice cream and watching people make a mess of their lives and/or remodel their kitchens.

The thing about being incredibly sad is that it's exhausting. I spend a lot of time sleeping. And standing around in the shower, just letting the hot water run over me until it feels like my skin will peel off.

You okay, Kooks? You've been in there for almost two hours.

Oh, really? Time flies when you're staring into space....

Whitlock Funeral Parlor takes care of everything funeral related, thank God, because I am completely nonfunctional. Mrs. Morris didn't have much in her savings, so we skip the rhinestones, and I have to say that the result is very tasteful.

All my friends come to the funeral. Brainzilla cries her guts out from the minute we get to the grave site. I've cried so much over the past three days that I feel all dried up, like there aren't any tears left in me.

My other friends didn't know Mrs. Morris that well, but they know how important she is…was…to me. We all hold hands as I read the letter I wrote. It's short. Here it is:

Eggy plays a really beautiful version of "Amazing Grace" on her trumpet. It's a cold day, but sunny and perfectly clear. An inch or two of snow fell overnight—just enough to cover the ground and make everything brilliant white. The crisp air feels good in my lungs. I don't cry, and I don't shatter like glass, though I feel like I might do either at any moment.

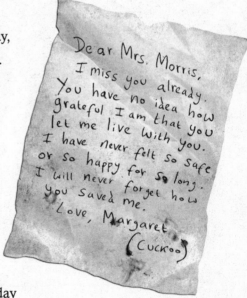

Dear Mrs. Morris,
I miss you already.
You have no idea how grateful I am that you let me live with you.
I have never felt so safe or so happy for so long.
I will never forget how you saved me.
Love, Margaret
(Cuckoo)

Is it right that such a sad day should be so beautiful?

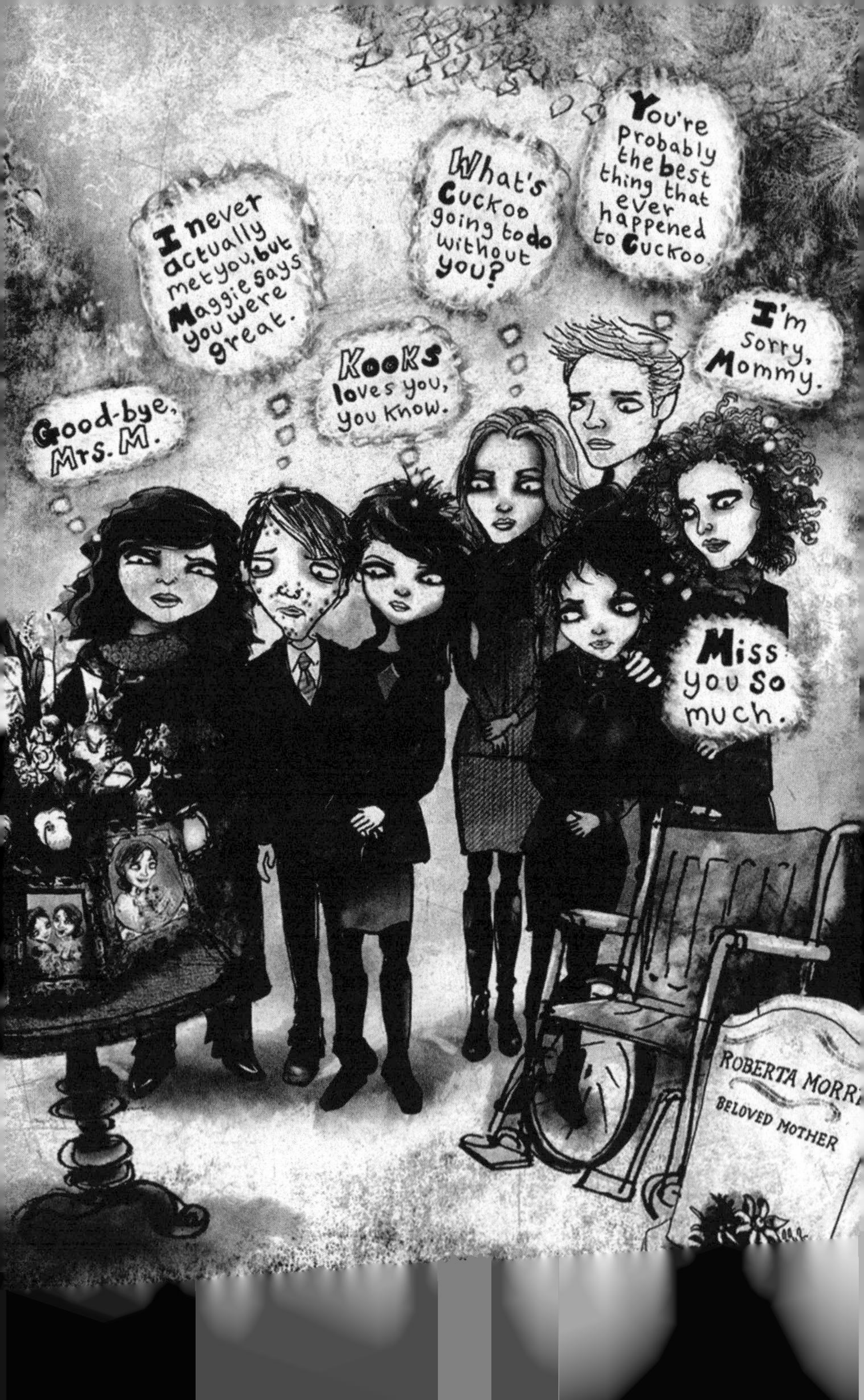

Good-bye, Mrs. M.
I never actually met you, but Maggie says you were great.
Kooks loves you, you know.
What's Cuckoo going to do without you?
You're probably the best thing that ever happened to Cuckoo.
I'm sorry, Mommy.
Miss you so much.
ROBERTA MORR
BELOVED MOTHER

A couple of days pass. Brainzilla can't tell if I'm just sad or having a crisis, so she calls Dr. Marcuse, and she and I have a long talk. By the end of it, Dr. Marcuse says I'm just sad, and I'm handling things very well, and I should come and talk to her next week, so we set up a time.

I don't mention my plan to stay in Mrs. Morris's house.

I don't think she'd support it, to tell you the truth. My friends sure don't.

But I really, really want to. Someone has to take care of Morris the Dog. Besides, I miss my room, even if it was only "mine" for a short time. I miss having a place that's mine, you know? Is this a good idea? Probably not. But what else am I supposed to do? Live with Brainzilla? Her family can barely afford the kids they have. Live with Eggy? Please—they're sweet, but they aren't looking for a new daughter.

Anyway, I figure I can stay at Mrs. Morris's for a little while....until Social Services comes after me.

It takes them only two days.

"Margaret Clarke?" the man asks.

I ask to see some identification, and Mr. Tenant Goldborough introduces himself. He's slim and losing his hair. In fact, he's losing his hair rapidly—in front of my very eyes. He walks around the living room, making notes in a small notebook and shedding all over the furniture. He seems kind of clueless, but mostly harmless. "Mrs. Morris was your care provider?"

"Yes."

"And the two of you lived here?"

"Yes."

Then he looks me in the eye and drops his bombshell.

"Ms. Clarke, I'm afraid that, as a minor, you can't live here alone." He's kind enough to look sort of sorry about it.

So I drop a bombshell right back.

"I'm not alone," I tell him.

Laurence and I are telling the truth.

Mrs. Morris's totally confused, utterly unreliable, super-flake twenty-something-or-other daughter, Marjorie, has been staying in the house with me ever since the funeral.

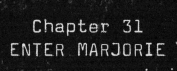

Hi, I'm Marjorie Morris. Have you seen my toast?

super flake

I think she was living with a few of her fellow flakes in California before this, but I'm not sure. Probably because she isn't too sure.

"I'm the adult here," Marjorie tells Mr. Goldborough in her awkward, quavering voice. He doesn't laugh, and neither do I, even though that's one of the craziest things I have ever heard—and I've spent time in a nuthouse.

No, instead Mr. Goldborough just nods and asks a few more questions, checks out Marjorie's ID, scribbles all the answers in his little notebook, and says he'll get back to her with a follow-up. In this one case, I'm actually kind of relieved the social service system is so sloppy and short on resources. To tell the truth, I think Mr. Goldborough is pretty relieved, too, that Marjorie showed up. I guess it isn't easy to find a placement for a sixteen-year-old with a (brief) history of mental problems.

"Do you plan to live here for the foreseeable future?" Mr. Goldborough asks.

"Oh, I can't see into the future," Marjorie tells him.

"Well, is it your plan to stay here?" he prompts.

"I try never to make plans," Marjorie replies. "Because they always change, don't they?"

Mr. Goldborough's pen hovers above the paper. "Well—will you be here awhile?"

"Absolutely." Marjorie checks her watch, as if a "while" might mean five minutes.

But Mr. Goldborough has heard the answer he needed and is already filling out paperwork. "Wonderful, wonderful. I'm glad this is going to work out," he says.

Hmm. I'm not sure it'll work out, but guess we'll see. Marjorie and I are in this together...for now. Talk about the confused leading the more confused.

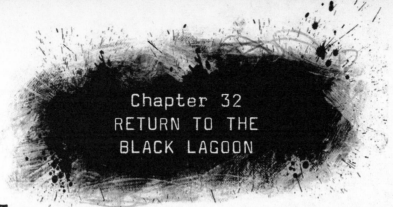

Chapter 32
RETURN TO THE
BLACK LAGOON

I round out the first week of the new year with my new housemate. It turns out that Marjorie has some hidden talents. She can play the piccolo. She is an excellent cook. And she never loses at cards—because she cheats.

She has had a pretty interesting life.

It's interesting to get to know her, but after four days, I'm feeling ready to get back to school.

I'm still spaced out, but I think a routine might help me. Sometimes *acting* normal is the best way to get back to *being* normal.

And, of course, I'm beyond thrilled to see my friends again. They seem happy to see me, too.

At lunch, I get a few cubes of fried tofu and something that I think is spinach before joining my friends at our usual table.

"Hey, Tebow," Zitsy is saying as I plunk down my tray, "I never heard how your trip to Guatemala went." Tebow and his church youth group spent Christmas building a library for some teeny-tiny town where there's nothing but coffee beans and Mayan ruins.

Tebow shrugs. "Got a nasty tapeworm. It was, like, five feet long when it came out."

"No good deed goes unpunished," Eggy says darkly.

Tebow seems unbothered by the fact that a giant worm was living in his gut. "Meh. It was kind of interesting. In a disgusting way."

"If you think that's disgusting, you should've seen the pipe I helped my dad clear on New Year's Eve," Zitsy announces.

Flatso holds up a hand. "I'm eating."

There's no way Zitsy's going to stop, though. "The clog was the size of a Chihuahua, and when it came loose, it spewed sewage everywhere! My dad looked like the Creature from the Crap Lagoon."

Flatso drops her spoon. "I can't even look at this stew."

"Subject change!" Brainzilla announces.

Eggy looks grateful. "Thank you."

"I've got an interview with an alum from—ahem!—*Yale University* in a week."

DUCK, Dad!

"They interview juniors?" Eggy's eyes bug in horror. "Oh, my God, are my parents going to want me to do that?"

"This is an informational interview," Brainzilla explains. "It's supposedly not a big deal, but I still have to figure out what to wear!"

"How about that Vera Wang wedding dress?" Tebow suggests.

And just like that, the Freakshow is off, suggesting outfits for Brainzilla's interview. Nobody seems to notice that I'm being almost completely silent, but at one point, Eggy slips her hand into mine and squeezes my fingers.

I'm happy to just be with them, surrounded by normal, as if I belong.

Chapter 33
MY BAD (AGAIN)

Margaret, I have been informed about the recent death of your caregiver, Mrs. Morris. I'm very sorry for your loss." Mr. Tool is facing me, but his eyes cling to the tidy pile of paperwork on his desk as he says this. He places a finger at his neck, like his tie is cutting off the blood flow to his head. It's interesting to watch the vice principal squirm.

I actually feel a tiny bit sorry for him, but I don't know what to say to make this moment less awkward.

He clears his throat, and the moment lingers. Now I feel like he's actually waiting for me to speak, which makes it even more impossible for me to think of anything to say. It's like a silence showdown. I wonder which one of us will break first.

Finally, I remember what people are supposed to say in this situation: "Thanks for your concern."

Mr. Tool nods, as if he's received the appropriate response and can now move on. "Ms. Kellerman is concerned that this situation may have caused a setback to your case."

I sigh. "Well, she should talk to Dr. Marcuse, who isn't concerned."

"It's perfectly natural that this would affect you, Margaret—"

"It *has* affected me." I have to fight tears, which are trying to strangle me.

"Given the fragile state of your mental health—"

"I'm sad, not crazy."

Mr. Tool cocks his head, then begins again, as if I haven't spoken. "Given the fragile state of your mental health—"

This is about all I can take from Mr. Tool. I really can't bear listening to the rest of this lecture, so I start playing a Lady Antebellum song in my head—that one where they drunk dial each other, all wasted and desperate.

I can't remember the rest of the words, so I switch to counting the hairs on my head. I feel a little bad for ignoring

Mr. Tool, but not very. (By the way, his name has been changed to punish the guilty. He's just...such an *implement*.)

After a while, Mr. Tool pauses, as if it's now my turn to speak.

"I'm sorry—what were you saying?" I lean forward in my chair a little, trying to look interested.

Mr. Tool sighs. "I guess we're through here, Margaret. I think we were through when we started."

"I'm really fine," I say as I haul myself out of the leather visitor's chair. I will say one thing for Mr. Tool—he has nice chairs. "Thanks for checking in. It was a really nice talk."

"Be careful out there."

"I know, it's a jungle."

"Yes...." He sighs and murmurs, "Sometimes it is."

Something about his tone makes me stop. Our gazes touch for a moment, and then his eyes shift back to the papers on his desk. But I realize suddenly that Mr. Tool really *is* afraid for me. He actually cares, in his own totally-not-effective way. He doesn't want to see me get eaten up.

For some reason, I find this almost tragic.

Chapter 34
HEY, CUCKOO CLARKE!

I'm not even halfway to my next class (bio with Winnie Quinn) when someone shoves me up against the metal lockers with a deafening clang.

I hear someone shout, "Hey!" from what seems like far away, but right here, right in my face, is Marty Bloom. His breath is so close I can smell the remains of his lunch. Sour-cream-and-onion potato chips and tuna-fish sandwich, for the record.

"You'd better not tell anyone about New Year's," he snarls, and it takes a moment for that to click into place for me.

"Bloom, I've got some serious problems right now," I tell him, "and you don't even make the list." He loosens his grip a bit—just enough so that the combination lock jamming into my back no longer feels like it's about to come out through my stomach.

Confusion flashes over Bloom's face, but before he can really process what I've said, Brainzilla slams into his shoulder.

"Leave Kooks alone, you dirtbag!" Brainzilla screams, clawing at his eyes.

"Get her off me!" Bloom shouts. "Get her off me!" He flaps at her like a five-year-old trying to shoo away a bee.

It strikes me that this moment isn't really very good for his image.

"Katie!" I try to pull her off Bloom, but don't get anywhere until Tebow and Flatso show up. The minute they pull Brainzilla off Bloom, he scrambles to his feet and lopes down the hall.

Tebow gapes at Brainzilla. "What was that all about?"

"Aren't we supposed to be nonviolent?" Flatso asks. "I thought that was your thing, Zilla."

Brainzilla's eyes flicker toward me, then narrow and follow

Bloom as he disappears down the hallway. Tebow is still watching her, waiting for an answer.

"Ask Kooks," she says at last.

Everyone looks at me, but I just shrug. Thankfully, nobody asks me to explain.

"Are you okay?" Tebow asks me.

"Yes," I say. It's true. I think.

I'm not really someone who advocates violence. Then again, it's nice to know that your friends have your back. So I'm not saying that what Brainzilla did was wrong...and I'm also not saying that I'm sorry she did it.

Flatso and I are working on an osmosis lab when the school secretary knocks on the doorframe. Winnie waves her in, and she hands him a note. He frowns as he reads it.

"Now?" Winnie asks Ms. Alter.

"That's what it says," the secretary snaps. She's always like that. I think she needs to stop drinking those giant Dunkin' Donuts coffees, because she is way irritable.

Winnie looks at me. "Kooks?"

The class stares at me as I gather my stuff and follow Ms. Alter out the door. She doesn't say where we're headed, but I can take a wild guess.

Ms. Kellerman looks up from her desk when I walk in. "Margaret—please sit down."

I plop into the chair across from hers. From the highly concerned look on her face, I guess my "progress" meeting with Mr. Tool didn't go all that well. From his point of view. That worries me a little. I don't want to get sent back to Crazytown. Can they do that?

"I am concerned, Margaret."

"Actually, it's Cuckoo." I shift my weight in the wooden chair. Ms. Kellerman's chairs aren't half as nice as Mr. Tool's. Maybe it's easier to get students to confess to things when they're uncomfortable.

The school psychologist smiles faintly. "I don't wish to make light of a serious situation."

"Really? Sometimes I think that's the best thing to do."

Ms. Kellerman looks at me like I'm a sentence she can't quite make sense of. Or maybe one of those word jumbles.

"In light of the recent developments in your case, I think it's time for you to show me your diary."

"No."

"I'm not asking. I *demand* to see it, Margaret." The corner of her mouth twists into a triumphant smile. "It's for your own safety."

"Nope."

Her smile falters. I think she really wasn't prepared for me to just flat-out refuse. But I can't figure out why she wants to see it so badly. She must think it's chock-full of crazy ramblings. I can't help thinking about how disappointed she would be by all my failed attempts to come up with a new ending for Twilight.

Maybe I should just show it to her. But don't I deserve a little privacy?

Just a shred?

You're back?" Winnie Quinn smiles when I walk up to his desk, but his eyes quickly cloud over.

"I just wanted to hand in the homework," I say, holding out my paper. The bell to end class has already rung, and there's chaos in the hallway. But Winnie must have this period free, because his classroom is empty.

"Are you okay, Cuckoo?" he asks as he takes my homework. He looks like he wants to say more, but he's not sure what. I remember that he probably has almost zero experience talking to other teenagers, because he spent his high school years in college.

I know we all kind of can't wait to get the hell out of here, but I don't think I'd want to have to be the youngest kid in the room all the time, like Winnie was.

"Oh, sure," I say. "I'm fine as can be. Fine as rain. Fine as angel-hair pasta. Fine as a lice comb! Couldn't be better. Top o' the mornin' to ya!" For some reason, I said that last thing in a really bad Irish accent. I don't know why I'm talking, and I can't imagine how awful I look right now, with puffy eyes and a drippy red nose.

I just spent twenty minutes arguing with Ms. Kellerman over

my diary, and I'm feeling pretty torn open and drained. I mean, I barely have enough energy to get out of bed in the morning, much less to fight with the school psychologist over privacy issues.

"Do you want to tell me what's going on?" Winnie asks. "Or not. I mean, I'm not asking like I'm a teacher and you have to tell me. I'm asking like a...person who's...concerned. If it'll help. If it won't, it's no big deal. Oh, sorry. I'm rambling again."

"It's okay," I say.

"Okay."

Silence fills up the space between us, and I'm grateful. Grateful that he cares enough to let me just be quiet for a while. Why do people think talking solves problems?

"I'm here if you ever change your mind," Winnie says finally.

That makes me feel like I might *really* talk to him someday. If I ever feel like talking again.

Right now, that's not looking too likely.

Chapter 37
FIRE IN THE HOLE!

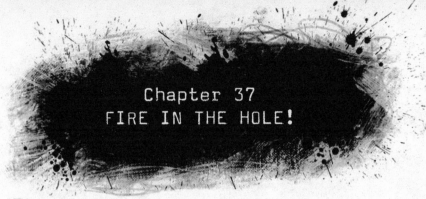

It's Monday, and usually Monday lunches are the best, because the cafeteria serves up ice cream. Sometimes they even have chocolate sauce and sprinkles. But my friends and I don't get to enjoy it, because Jenna McClue decides to serve up a fight instead.

"You bitch!" she screams, right in Brainzilla's face. "You made out with my boyfriend!"

"Bloom?" Brainzilla gives Jenna this cool, lifted-eyebrow look that most people find super-intimidating. "Does he know he's supposed to be your boyfriend?"

I fight the urge to crouch behind a piece of furniture. I don't know what Jenna heard—but it must have been about me, not Brainzilla. Jenna doesn't even glance in my direction, though. She just stares at Brainzilla's lifted eyebrow as if she wants to rip it off.

Brainzilla frowns, like she feels sorry for Jenna. "Look, I hate to tell you this, but your so-called boyfriend has—"

"Stop talking!" Jenna screeches, just before she lunges at my best friend. Suddenly—it's *on*.

Brainzilla is losing, big time! Jenna has wrapped her fingers in Brainzilla's hair and is yanking like she's trying to get the top

off a cheap wine cooler. Brainzilla lets out a scream, and I don't even have time to think—I just jump in and bite Jenna's arm.

"She bit me!" Jenna is shrieking like a car alarm bent on revenge, but the minute she lets go of Brainzilla's hair and comes after me, Flatso dives in and holds her off.

Tebow grabs Jenna and delivers her—still screeching—to a group of stunned Barbies. "Stay away from him!" Jenna screams. "Stay away from my boyfriend!"

Brainzilla's fingers are covering her eye. I can tell it's swollen from where Jenna's fist caught her right under the brow bone. "Don't worry, I will!" Zilla snarls.

And there's a moment—just a tiny moment—when I should say, "She never went near him! That was me—Bloom tried to attack me!" But the moment slips by, and Flatso steps forward and wraps a thick arm protectively around Brainzilla's shoulder.

"Come on," Flatso says gently.

The entire cafeteria is silent as Flatso steers us all toward the door. Everyone stares—I feel their eyes like fingers poking at me.

"Get me out of here," Brainzilla whispers. I catch my best friend's spare hand, and Eggy takes up the rear. We're just heading to the girls' room, but I feel like we're escorting a prisoner to the cellblock.

Nobody harass the prisoner— she's potentially violent!

What the hell is *wrong* with people?" Brainzilla wails once we're behind closed doors. She, Eggy, and I are crammed into the handicap stall of the girls' bathroom. I put down a huge mass of paper towels all over the toilet, just in case anyone needs to sit down. Flatso stands in front of the locked stall door to make double sure nobody comes in.

"Oh, Zilla," Eggy says, pulling her close. Brainzilla's tears leak onto Eggy's shoulder. Eggy's tears pour into Brainzilla's hair. My tears spill down my face and fall into my lap. (Yes, I'm the one sitting on the toilet.) And Flatso's tears trickle straight into the corners of her mouth.

"My nose is pouring snot all over your sweater," Brainzilla says.

"I *love* snot," Eggy swears.

Brainzilla holds out her hand to me, and I squeeze it. She has a massively swelling eye, and her hands are shaking. I press her fingers to my cheek. "People have been mean to me before," she says. "But I've never been—attacked." She gulps for air, and her tears start to flow again.

I know how she feels. Having someone go after you like that—for no reason, or for a reason that isn't even real—it messes with your sense of safety. I remember Bloom, the fear I felt when I was shut into that small car with him and thought

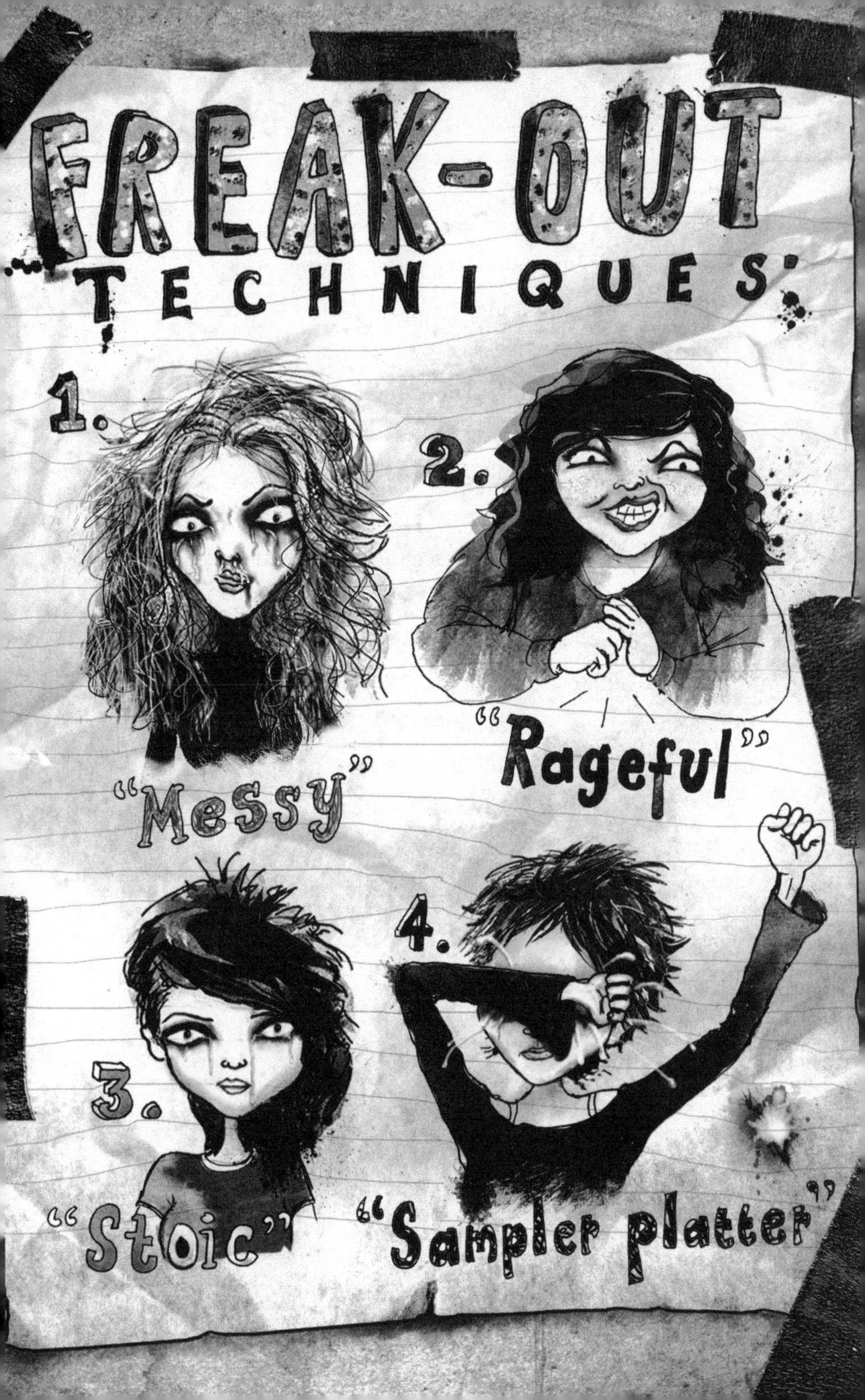
FREAK-OUT
TECHNIQUES
1.
"Messy"
2.
"Rageful"
3.
"Stoic"
4.
"Sampler platter"

I'd never get out—

"I hate those Haters for making me cry," Eggy says, smashing her knuckles into her eyes. "I never cry!"

"If Jenna tries anything again, I'll pound her into hamburger," Flatso promises.

"That's just it!" Brainzilla cries. "No pounding! I'm all about nonviolence! But the Haters—they're making me into the guy from *The Texas Chainsaw Massacre*!"

She sobs again, and Flatso looks like someone has just ripped her heart out, and I'm feeling so low I'm practically at the center of the earth.

This is all my fault. Bloom tried to make out with *me*, not Brainzilla. Jenna should've mistakenly tried to claw *my* eyes out. And yes! I know that doesn't make sense! Neither one of us is after Jenna's boyfriend, so what difference does it make, right? But still—I should've said something, even though it probably just would've made everything more confusing. My heart is skittering like it can't get a foothold, and then, before I even know what I'm doing, I hear myself say, "Knock, knock."

Silence, except for the sound of breathing.

"What?" Brainzilla says after a moment.

I clear my throat. "Um…I said, 'Knock, knock.'"

Eggy's voice is tentative. "Who's there?"

"Hater."

"Hater, who?" Flatso asks.

"Hey, dere!" I say in a really bad Italian accent. "Woulda you lika some lasagna?"

Everyone stares at me for a moment.

It's a long moment.

Yep, still going.

Finally, Brainzilla sniffs. "Hey, dere," she says slowly. "That was totally the worst joke I've ever heard."

Eggy's chuckle comes out as a snort. "Hey, dere," she puts in. "I thinka we needa to senda you backa to Crazytown."

Flatso wipes the tears from her face. "Hey, dere. You guys are *so* sweet that we'll have to forgive you for butchering those Italian accents."

I shook my head. "I know. That was terrible. I'm sorry!"

"Hey, dere. Give me a hug, you coconuts," Brainzilla says, and we pile on for a big arm-fest. "You're a good friend," she says into my hair.

"I'm not," I reply. "I'm always all wrapped up in my own problems."

Brainzilla and I look at each other.

"Who said that?" Eggy calls.

"It's me," says a familiar voice. "Zitsy."

"Zitsy!" Flatso cries. She unbars the door and swings it open. Zitsy is sitting on a sink. "What are you doing in the girls' bathroom? You can't be in here!"

"Bathrooms have no secrets from me," Zitsy says. "Unfortunately."

I just feel like the bad guys are winning," Zitsy says. "I feel it just eating away at me, the way Drano eats away at a hair clog. I just walk around all day, wondering why someone like Jenna is rich, while Brainzilla has to work her ass off—"

Tears fill his eyes, and Flatso hands him a long strand of toilet paper. Zitsy's crying so much I'm afraid we might need a boat to get out of this girls' room.

"Thank you." Zitsy blows his nose. "And Bloom is mean to everyone, but it's Kooks who gets sent to a mental hospital. A mental hospital! Are you kidding me?" He looks at Eggy. "And then I think about those guys who called you names—"

"Don't," Eggy says, putting up her arms.

"They treated you like you were a piece of garbage! But *they're* the garbage!" And Zitsy dissolves into tears.

Hana has her arms wrapped around her shins and her face pressed against her knees. Her back shakes a bit, and I rub my hand over her soft sweater.

"I just don't know how much more I can stand!" Zitsy wails, and bursts into tears all over again.

"It's good that you can share your feelings," Brainzilla tells him.

"Yeah, Zitsy," Flatso agrees. "I guess that's why they always say 'you're such a girl.'"

"That's why we love you," I add, but it's too late—he's already offended.

"I'm a total guy," Zitsy insists. "I'm gonna be a plumber, for god's sake."

"That's the *other* reason we love you," I tell him. "Everybody needs a good plumber."

Chapter 40
TERROR, INC.

I barely register being in math class. I have no
idea what Mrs. Rosewater is saying. Usually,
being a Terror Teacher, she loves to call on people
who seem sleepy or spaced out. But I spend the
entire class with my eyes glazed, just staring
out the window, and she doesn't call on me
once, or even tell me to pay attention.

I watch a squirrel leap from branch
to branch, shaking snow to the white
ground with every step. Some of
it blows away in the wind, like a
ghost.

The bell rings, and I snap back
into this world. I gather up my books
and think I'm about to get out alive
when Mrs. Rosewater says,
"Margaret, would you
please stay a moment?"

This is it, I think as I walk up to her desk. *She's going to scream at me for not paying attention, take points off my grade, report me to Mr. Tool—*

"I was so sorry to hear about Roberta's passing," Mrs. Rosewater says. She reaches for my hand. "She was my student, you know."

And I'm thinking, *Who's Roberta? Who's Roberta?* And then it hits me—Mrs. Rosewater is talking about Mrs. Morris, and it catches me so off guard that tears spring to my eyes.

"She was always a very conscientious student—and very kind. Is someone taking care of Morris?"

"The dog?" I ask, and Mrs. Rosewater nods. Wow. Mrs. Morris and Mrs. Rosewater kept in touch? I'm so surprised that I actually answer her question. "I am. Well, and Marjorie, too. She and I are staying at the house together."

"Ah! That's good." Mrs. Rosewater nods and squeezes my fingers. "Very good."

"Well, DSS says I need someone to look after me," I explain.

"Is that what's going on?" Mrs. Rosewater laughs. "I wonder who will end up looking after whom." She sighs. "Roberta would be so happy to know Marjorie is back at the house."

"Were you good friends?" I ask.

"We would have coffee once in a while. I don't know if she told you, but Roberta used to babysit my children back when I was her teacher." She takes out a wallet and pulls a worn photo from it.

I'm *fall-on-the-floor* surprised. It's her, a younger Mrs. Morris, and three kids. I never thought about Mrs. Rosewater being someone's mother...or someone's friend.

"She was so happy when you came to live with her," Mrs. Rosewater tells me. "She worried about you, though."

"I was lucky to have her," I say. Then, seeing the concern on my teacher's face, I add, "I'm really, honestly making progress. I'm doing the best I can."

"I know that, Margaret." Mrs. Rosewater is still holding my hand. Her fingers are warm. She doesn't look away from me.

I have no idea what makes me do this, but I pull my diary out of my backpack. "Do you want to see something funny?" I ask her. "You have to promise not to tell Ms. Kellerman."

Mrs. Rosewater rolls her eyes. "I wouldn't even tell that woman if her own pants were on fire. I'm certainly not going to go blabbing about you."

The good thing about having something horrible happen is that you realize that people actually care about you. The bad thing is that having so much care and concern can feel a little overwhelming.

And all the concern at school is making me feel a little bit nutso at home. Having Marjorie around is only adding to the nuttiness factor.

For one thing, she keeps vampire hours: awake from twilight to sunrise, asleep most of the day. For another thing, she's obsessed with the Home Shopping Network. She never buys anything—she just sits on the couch, hating on everything they bring out.

And to top things off, Morris the Dog makes her sneeze. "I'm allergic to dander," she explains.

So I walk Morris, and give him baths, and vacuum the house to get rid of dander. Marjorie takes care of the cooking. Neither one of us is very good at taking out the garbage. We're managing, but I sometimes feel as if I'm hanging on by my fingernails.

Everyone's so worried about my progress that I start to worry that I'm not making any. Am I? I *did* cry in Ms. Kellerman's office, which can't be good. And I've felt really shaky ever since the fight....

Am I backsliding? Frontsliding? I never really thought I was crazy to begin with. What if I was? How would I know?

This is the kind of thinking that can turn you crazy, if you aren't already.

If I were Brainzilla or Eggy, I could ask my mom if she ever felt this way and how she got through it. But I'm not them. I have no idea if my mom ever felt crazy. I only know the most basic stuff about her life.

Mom's Life

(I never met them.)

Born of hippies.

Raised in a commune in Idaho.

Couple of years in Eugene at UO. Falls in love.

Daddy Splits on Mommy and Cuckoo.

Mom splits on Cuckoo. And Cuckoo Splits.

Good as new. I'm fine. (Not really, Mom. Let's talk. Mom? Are you out there? Are you anywhere?)

Steri-strips

Gets glued back together.

?????

Entenmann's?" Brainzilla asks when I open the door. She's holding out a box of chocolate-covered doughnuts.

"I've got milk!" Flatso says, holding up a gallon. "Plus three Will Ferrell movies!"

"Oh, I—"

"We thought we'd have a sleepover," Brainzilla says as she pushes open the door. "If you don't mind." She and Flatso don't wait for me to agree, or anything. They just bust into the living room, where Marjorie is drinking coffee in her bathrobe and cursing out an electric knife on TV.

"Listen, guys, I'm not sure that Marjorie—"

"Did someone say Entenmann's?" Marjorie asks.

My friends charm Marjorie, who gets dressed and makes us a pesto-and-gorgonzola pizza (which is delicious, by the way).

Later, when Marjorie heads out to go grocery shopping at midnight (her favorite time), I get to have some quality time with my besties. We settle in and flip through magazines, while Flatso paints our toenails. My room is still cold, but it feels cozy with my friends and Morris to cheer me up.

"I'm so glad you two came over tonight."

"Yeah—we kind of thought you needed a hug," Flatso says.

Brainzilla nods.

I swear—my friends are the best. I couldn't even make up anyone as good as them.

"I don't know how you guys even put up with me," I say. I seriously mean this. Who wants to be friends with someone who's sad all the time?

"We love you," Flatso says. "And the thing is, you don't even understand how amazing you are."

"W. H. Auden was talking about *you* when he said poetry is 'the formation of private spheres out of a public chaos,'" Brainzilla replies.

"Thanks," I whisper. I'm not really sure what she means, but I think she's talking about my writing. Anyway, I know she means it as a compliment, and I love her for just being here. And for being her.

I know I've had a lot of bad luck lately. But I've had good luck, too.

Just look at how lucky I am right now.

This is Hana. You know my mom doesn't let me do sleepovers, but I'm there in spirit. I love you, Kooks.

Three hours.

That's how long it took Brainzilla to decide what to wear to her informational interview with the Yale alum. I didn't realize that it was possible for one person to own so many accessories.

Once we narrow down the choices, Brainzilla comes out looking gorgeous and impressive, as always. She's wearing a soft pink sweater and a gray knit skirt. Black tights and high-heeled booties make her legs look five miles long, and she has on a wrist full of funky African bangles made by a women's cooperative that she did a fund-raiser for last year. (Perfect conversation starter.) Even though this isn't a super-official interview, Brainzilla always goes for the knockout punch. Still, she's so nervous that she begs me to come with her to the café.

"Won't that look weird?" I ask.

"I'm not asking you to sit in my lap," Brainzilla says. "Just walk with me, so I don't hyperventilate and die on the way there. Then you can order a Frappuccino and read, or whatever, while I talk to this woman."

She had me at "Frappuccino."

She also would've had me at "muffin," "biscotti," or "hot cocoa." I'm kinda easy, I guess.

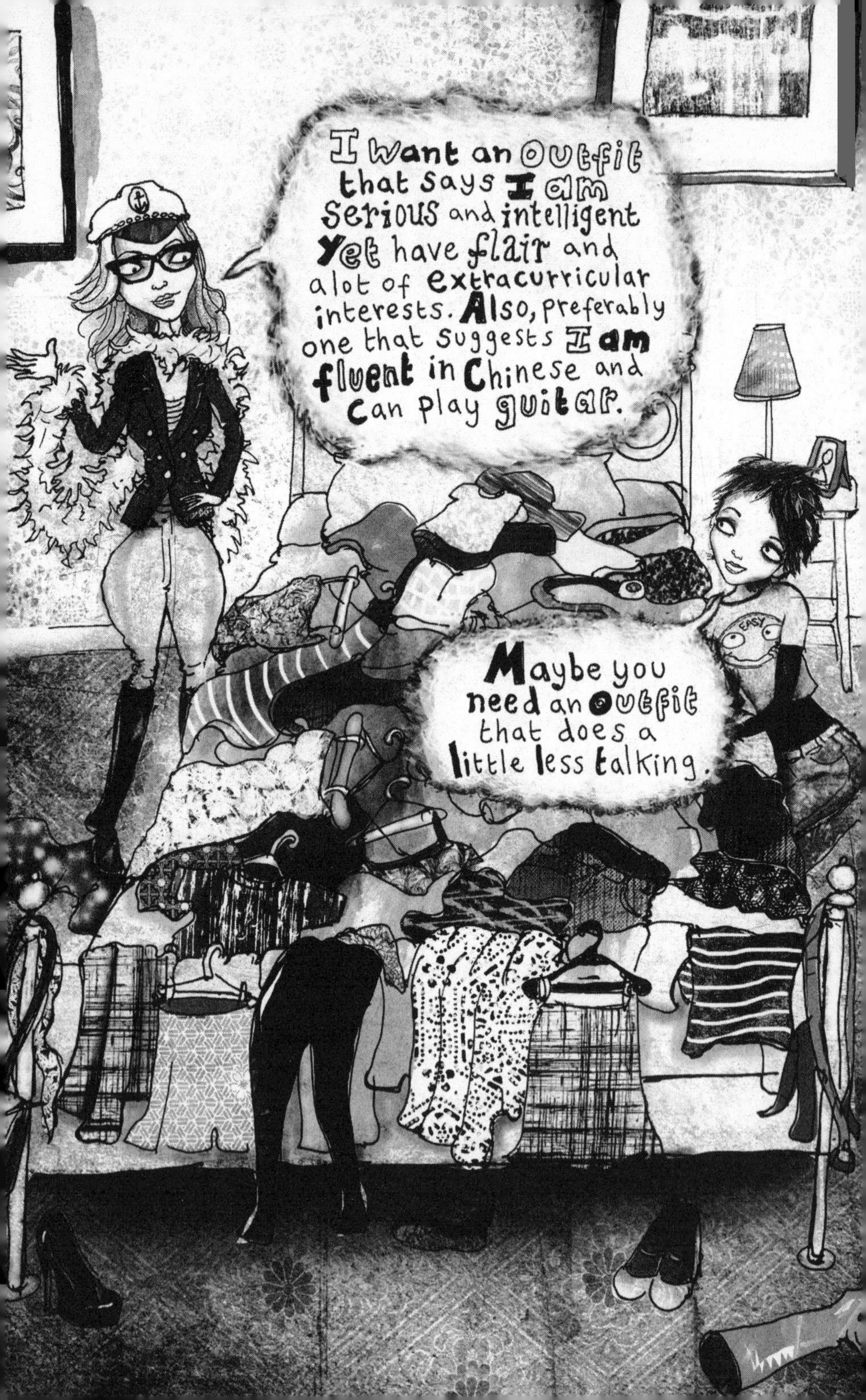
I want an outfit that says I am serious and intelligent yet have flair and alot of extracurricular interests. Also, preferably one that suggests I am fluent in Chinese and can play guitar.
Maybe you need an outfit that does a little less talking.
EASY

But before we reach the front door, Brainzilla's mom calls, "Katie!" She dashes in, her hair escaping in wisps from her ponytail. In her brown Cape Cod sweatshirt and jeans, she looks younger than Brainzilla. "How long will you be gone?"

"Just an hour, Mom," Brainzilla promises.

"I really need your help with your brothers," Mrs. Sloane says.

"Just an hour." Brainzilla is begging, and I wonder if her mother even knows where she's going. Her parents didn't go to college. The whole idea is vague to them—except for the cost, which is real, and terrifying.

But Mrs. Sloane just nods, and Brainzilla and I walk out the door. Even though I'm supposed to be keeping her calm, we're silent the three blocks to the café. I let Brainzilla walk in first, then slink into the warm, fragrant air like an innocent bystander. I order my drink and settle in at a table beside a steamed-up window.

Brainzilla's feet are tap-tap-tapping beneath her table, so I know she's nervous. But even from across the café, I can tell that she and the Yale lady are getting along well. Zilla gestures wildly, and Yale Lady laughs. Perfect.

I space out and look around the café. I didn't bring a book— or even my notebook—so I decide to play my favorite form of solitaire. It's a game I made up in which I imagine the people around me as literary characters.

This is such a fun game that I completely lose track of time, and before I know it, Brainzilla has slipped into the seat across from mine. She's beaming so hugely that I don't even need to ask how it went. But I'm polite.

"How was it?"

"Fabulous!" Brainzilla peeks over her shoulder, but the woman has disappeared into the parking lot. "We really got along."

"You can talk to anyone."

"I even told her to friend me, so we can stay in touch on Facebook," Brainzilla gushes. "I wanted her to see the photos from debate team, and a few from the hospital." Brainzilla has a volunteer gig reading stories to kids with cancer. Because she has so much spare time.

She reaches across the table and grabs my hand. "I can just feel it, Kooks! This is the beginning of the beginning!" Her toes are still tapping a crazy dance beneath the table, as if a thousand volts of electricity are shooting through her. I know she's happy, but I can tell by her wide eyes that she's stressed out.

"That's great!" I really want to tell her that I'm proud of her, but that's kind of silly. I mean, even with perfect grades and excellent test scores, and a million extracurriculars, she still might not get into Yale. I know she's counting on it. I know she thinks her whole life will change if she goes to an Ivy League school.

I just hope it works out the way she hopes it will.

I think we're all kind of counting on it.

Some people have video games, some have bad reality television, and I have homeroom with Laurence.

There's nothing wrong with escaping from reality sometimes. It's not like I'm a heroin addict.

Well, I might be a *heroine* addict, or in Laurence's case, a *hero* addict, but that's not as dangerous. So I don't hesitate to imagine up a lovely date with Laurence. Dating him is way easier than dating in real life. Real life is complicated.

Friends?
More than friends?
What's the meaning of this?

Potential criminal.
Hatemonger.
Handsome, though.

Teacher?
More than a teacher?
Another quandary.

Handsome, brilliant, and adores me.
Also: disappears on command.

Ding, ding, ding!

DATING = COMPLICATED

LOVE

LOVE

KOOKS + BLOOM

BLOOMING CUCKOO!!

'Mrs Maggie Cuckoo' Quirin

MR.DARCY!!

KOOKS 4EVA

ESCAPE FROM REALITY

Laurence

KOOKS

Real life = Complicated

TEBOW   BLOOM   WINNIE   LAURENCE

Laurence's only flaw is that he doesn't exist.

"Your only flaw is that you *do* exist," Laurence tells me. Sigh—high school boys never come up with such witty repartee!

I can't tell you how much I love thinking about Laurence and writing down our story. With Laurence, I can have our first kiss take place under a rainbow or in a cave hidden behind a waterfall or up in a hot-air balloon. Whatever I want—I'm in charge. I'm not in charge of much these days, but I am in charge of that.

Laurence and I go for a stroll in the summer countryside. It's warm and smells like hay. Dust motes float on golden sunshine as he tells me that he loves me. He says that he wants us to be together forever, in a comfortable house with a small garden in the back.

Everything is beautiful and wonderful for fifteen minutes. Then the bell rings, and I have to plunge back into the daily grind.

Reality is way overrated.

Chapter 45
HOW LOW CAN WE GO?

Oh, no," Brainzilla breathes an hour later. Her face is pale, and her feet are doing their crazy stress dance beneath her desk.

"What's wrong?" I ask, reaching out to touch her shoulder.

"I didn't study," she whispers. "I'm a little behind in the reading." We're in English class, and Ms. Olsson is handing out pop quizzes.

Ms. Olsson just looooooooves pop quizzes.

"How far behind?"

Ridiculous Pop Quiz Mountain: practically impossible to climb!

I have a surprise for you, class! And I know how much you **love** surprises!

Is it cupcakes?

Even better!

Brainzilla's eyes flash at me. "I had to prep for my interview, Kooks." Her voice is brittle, like a word might break off and land on her foot.

"It's okay," I say to Brainzilla. "It's just one test."

"You don't understand," she hisses, shaking her head at me. "You don't know what it takes to get into a school like Yale." Brainzilla mashes her lips together, and her breathing comes fast and shallow from her nose.

"You'll do fine," I say, trying to sound encouraging. "At least you haven't fallen asleep, like Tebow. Wake up!" I lean forward to whisper in his ear. Tebow's head is bowed, his eyes closed.

"Shh!" He opens one eye and glares at me with it, then snaps it closed again. His lips start to move, but I can't hear what he's saying.

"Stop that!" I hiss. "What are you doing? Silas Marner is coming to get you!" Ugh. Sorry to be a mini Hater, but I despise *Silas Marner*. If you're a fan, please contact me via my Twitter handle @silassux and explain why this is great literature. Warning: I may use your answer on a pop quiz.

Tebow's lips stop moving, and he opens his eyes just as Sheila McGuinness hands back the pile of quizzes. "As long as there are tests, there will be prayer in public schools," he explains.

"Pray for me, too," Brainzilla says. She doesn't sound like she's kidding.

"Done," Tebow says, snapping his eyes shut and muttering to himself.

"Mr. Jemowicz!" Ms. Olsson shrieks. It takes me a minute to remember that Jemowicz is Tebow's real last name. "This will be your first and last warning! I expect SILENCE!"

There's something funny about hearing the word *silence* screamed at top volume, but I don't dare laugh, because Ms. Olsson's got her Crazy Teacher face on. I swear, that woman needs a ten-day observation period at St. Auggie's way more than I ever did.

Here is the difference between Mrs. Rosewater and Ms. Olsson, which I didn't even realize until Mrs. R. revealed that she's an actual human being:

Mrs. Rosewater is strict.

Ms. Olsson is *mean*. She loves giving pop quizzes because she likes to see us squirm—and fail.

You know what they say: Misery loves company. I guess Ms. Olsson is as miserable as they come, because she loves to make us suffer.

I blew it," Brainzilla says when we reach gym class. "I totally blew that test." She inhales slowly, then nearly gags. The gym smells like an old sneaker dipped in swamp juice, so it's not exactly ideal for deep, relaxing breaths.

"It was just a quiz," I point out. "She gives us, like, two a week—so it's only worth about one-fiftieth of our grade."

"Still—a zero could bring my grade down to a B." My best friend tucks her hair behind her ears in a nervous gesture that I know well. "And a B isn't getting me a scholarship to Yale. And now we have dodgeball." She shudders and refrains from taking in another relaxing meditation inhale.

Dodgeball is the moment when the Haters get to slam rubber balls at us with impunity. It's Freakshow torture.

"Sloane! Clarke!" Mrs. McGrath—the gym teacher—points to the far wall. "Line up!"

"Um, Mrs. McGrath—could Brainzilla and I just run laps?" I ask.

"This is a *dodgeball* unit," Mrs. McGrath snarls. "Line up."

"But—" I glance over at Brainzilla, who doesn't look like she can handle a battle. "Look—running is better exercise than dodgeball," I protest.

"This is a dodgeball unit," Mrs. McGrath repeats.

Brainzilla just shakes her head and starts for the wall. "Forget trying to reason with her," she mutters.

I consider telling Mrs. McGrath that dodgeball is against my religion.

But I know she'll probably just send me to see Mr. Tool—or worse, Ms. Kellerman. In the end, it just seems easier to get whacked by a bunch of balls.

We get clobbered a couple hundred times, and I spend the next fifty minutes fuming about how completely unreasonable it is to make people play dodgeball against their will. It isn't even a sport in the Olympics! (Is it? I'd better Google that.)

(Googled it—it isn't!)

Also, it's unreasonable to make students take pop quizzes twice a week.

Also, it's unreasonable to demand to see someone's diary!

And at the end of class, while I'm changing back into my jeans, I realize something: This school is completely unreasonable, and that's why everyone is so miserable!

Which leads me straight to my next thought: Let's get reasonable!

I can't wait to share that idea with the Freakshow—just as soon as I change out of my gross gym clothes and exit the swamp-juice-smell area.

Brainzilla jumps on the idea. Maybe she wants to make up for her blown quiz, or maybe she sees an opportunity for a few cool Facebook pics to impress her Yale friend with. Either way, she's all over the Rally for Reason. "Yes! Stop the hate!" Brainzilla announces. She whips out a notebook and starts to jot down a few calculations. "Okay, there are fifteen hundred students at the school, and a good participation rate would be about eighty percent...."

"Should we charge an entrance fee?" Eggy asks. "We could raise money for a good cause."

Tebow tugs on his lower lip. "No—we want everyone to be able to participate. Not just people who can afford it."

"We'll talk about how ridiculous this school is!" I say, and I can feel myself glowing with this idea. I imagine all the Nations coming together, sharing our ideas about how to make the teachers and administration more reasonable. Then I imagine *everyone* feeling better—whether or not the teachers change anything.

"We could rewrite the school regulations," Flatso suggests. "And get rid of that ridiculous rule saying we can't wear glitter nail polish."

"Let people opt out of dodgeball!" I cry. "And pop quizzes should only be given in cases of emergency!"

"What about that ban on hugging?" Zitsy puts in. Wow— I'd forgotten about that, but he's right. Hugs are technically forbidden on campus. That was Mr. Tool's brilliant brainstorm our freshman year.

"Jeez, no wonder everyone's stressed out," Tebow says. "Maybe we could suggest a few moments for prayer—or, like, meditation or whatever—during homeroom. Optional, of course."

"I'll do a flyer," Eggy volunteers.

"I'll organize the water and snacks for everyone," Zitsy puts in.

And just like that, we finally have an Operation Happiness idea that might actually work.

Chapter 47
WE GO LOWER

By the end of the next day, the Freakshow has papered the entire school with rally flyers. Eggy did such a great job designing them that we (okay, I) got really excited and may have gone a little overboard.

As of last period, I'd seen three people take copies of the flyer, and only one of them was using it to toss out her gum. Success!

Meanwhile, Brainzilla got busy laying out three alternate scenarios, estimating the likely size of the crowd based on weather, time of day, and whether we experienced resistance from some of the Nations. And once the rally was over, Eggy would deejay a dance party on the front lawn!

I feel like anything could happen, and that feeling lasts all the way through the final bell and out into the parking lot. The Freakshow and I are headed toward Zitsy's car when I notice Marty Bloom staring at our flyer. He's with his best friend/sidekick/henchman, Stoors.

"Join hands and share ideas?" Bloom makes a retching noise.

"Rip it down, man," Stoors says.

So Bloom does. And just as I hear the paper tear away from the lamppost, Bloom looks up at me...and smiles.

The good feeling that has buoyed me all day dries up and crumbles.

"Put that back!" Eggy shrieks, but Bloom has already torn the flyer in half.

"Why don't you stuck-up, perfect people go sing 'Kumbaya' somewhere else?" Bloom sneers. "Stop trying to spread your feel-good PC bullshit in everyone's face."

Brainzilla's face has turned pale, but she stands her ground.

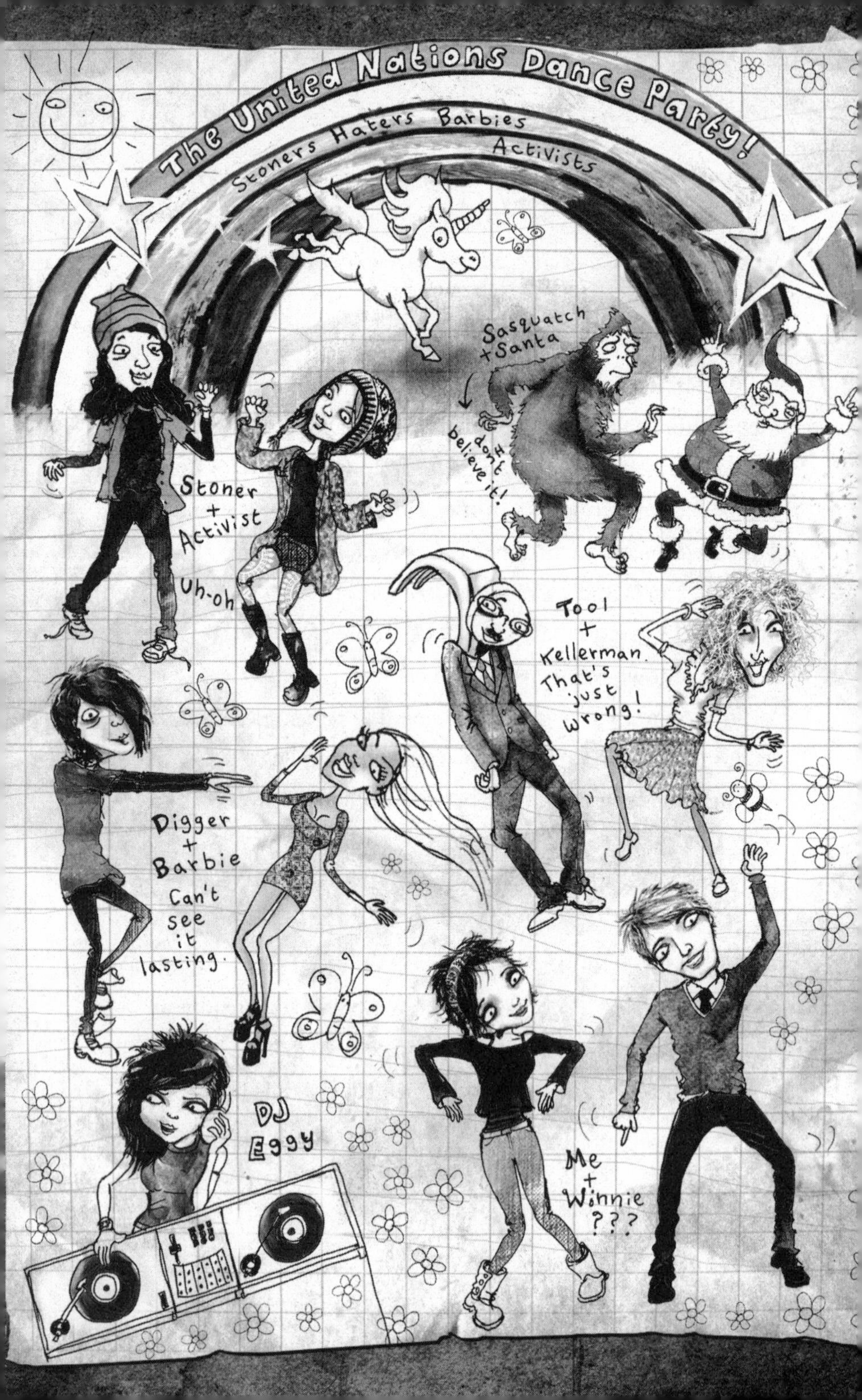

The United Nations Dance Party!
Stoners Haters Barbies
Activists
Sasquatch + Santa
don't believe it!
Stoner + Activist
Uh-oh
Tool + Kellerman. That's just wrong!
Digger + Barbie
Can't see it lasting.
DJ Eggy
Me + Winnie ???

Still, her voice is quiet when she says, "It isn't bullshit to want to do something positive."

"Shut up, slut," Stoors snaps. "Or I'll have someone else claw your eyes out."

The memory of Jenna's attack flashes through my mind, and I see Brainzilla flinch. We aren't the only ones remembering the fight—I have to dive in front of Flatso, who had just barreled toward the Haters with—I believe—foul intentions.

"Don't even think of threatening her!" Tebow shouts, and Bloom says, "Why don't you try to stop me?" and I'm thinking that stuff is about to get seriously out of hand when Winnie Quinn appears and demands, "What's going on here?"

In the silence that follows, I realize how crowded and still the parking lot is. Nobody is getting in a car to leave. Everyone is just watching us, as stationary as the lamppost beside me.

Winnie eyes the torn flyer in Bloom's hand. "Did you take that down? Why would you do that?"

Bloom's only response is a sneer, but it bounces off Winnie like bullets off Superman's chest.

"These people," Winnie says, pointing at us—well, really, at me, "are just trying to do something positive. If you don't want to do it, fine. You don't have to. But you don't have to ruin things for everyone else, either." He turns to face the gawkers. "And why don't any of you speak up?"

Nobody says anything, which seems to irritate Winnie even more. "God! I'm so sick of stupid bullies ruining everything!"

He points at Bloom. "You don't get to decide what everyone else does! Now, apologize!"

Bloom crosses his arms and smirks. "Or what? You can't really believe you have any kind of authority in this place. You're just another weirdo like the rest of them—no idea how to just be *normal*."

Winnie looks like he's been punched. But just as I think he's about to back off, he gets right in Bloom's face.

"I'd rather be like the rest of them than some spoiled rich kid who pretends he's happy but never gets enough attention from Daddy and doesn't have any real friends because they're all just using him for his money. I'd rather be one of *these* kids any day. In fact, I *am* one of these kids! Now. *Apologize!*"

And to my shock, Bloom's face has gone pale. He mutters something that might or might not be an apology, but either way, he takes off, and Stoors follows. Then Winnie stomps to his MINI Cooper before anyone can say a word.

I call out, "Thank you!" but I don't think he hears me—he's already pulling away.

"That was so heroic," Flatso murmurs with a wink and a laugh. She had given up on her crush on Winnie almost instantly, and then it became sort of an inside joke. But I wholeheartedly agree that Winnie is basically a superhero. It crosses my mind that I may be falling in love with Winnie Quinn. That may sound absurd and childish, but I don't even care. It feels nice. And I've never been in love before. Except with Laurence.

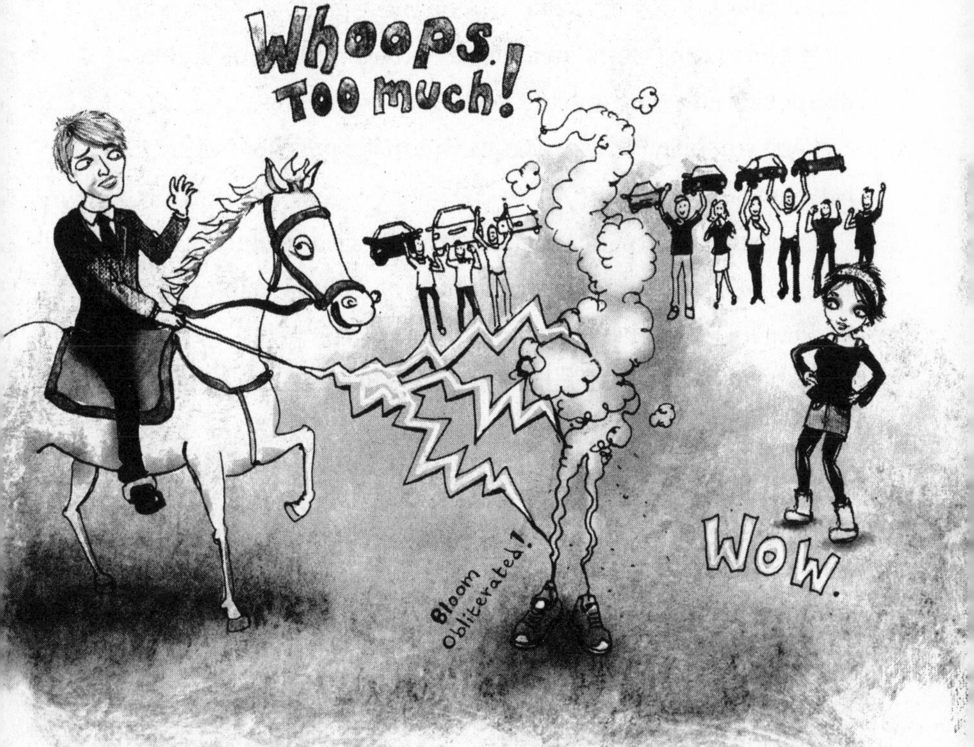
Whoops. Too much!
Bloom obliterated!
WOW.

Brainzilla sits down, right down on the asphalt in the parking lot, like she can't stand up a moment longer. My good feeling disappears into the air, like a soap bubble popping.

"Are you okay?" Zitsy asks as Brainzilla puts her head between her knees.

I put my hand on her back and realize she's shaking. Brainzilla is a tiny earthquake, quivering right here in the parking lot. "It's okay," I tell her.

"It's *not* okay," Brainzilla whispers. She wipes her hands down her face, then looks up at me. There are shadows deep as bruises under her blue eyes, and I wonder if she has been sleeping. Her pale skin and delicate features make her look fragile.

"Don't worry." I kneel down next to Brainzilla, ignoring the gravel that bites into my knees. "We'll bring the Nations together, and the Haters will come around."

"Will they?" Brainzilla's expression is flat, as if she doesn't believe a word I'm saying. "Or will he just have someone try to beat me up again?"

My friends look at each other. I guess we're all a little unsure. Brainzilla has always been so strong, but it looks like the increasingly tense situation with Bloom has left her feeling—well, scared, I guess. It's as if she's made of china and might shatter at any moment.

It's confusing. Isn't she the one who's supposed to have it all together?

Wait. I thought I was the one who was falling apart.

I gh fwabwagh arg dey." Marjorie takes a huge, hiccupy breath and then starts speaking this weird alien language again. "I can't blurgreve!"

Marjorie is crying her eyes out. She's been this way since I walked through the front door, and I can't understand a word she's saying, but I'm trying really hard to be sympathetic. I would be more sympathetic if I knew what the hell was going on. Marjorie babbles some more, and I hope she's not having a stroke. She's a little young for it, but still....

"Oh, Kooks!" she wails.

"It'll be okay," I tell her. Poor thing.

"You're so strong!" She mashes her lips together, and now I really have the feeling I don't know what's going on.

"Really, I'm sure it's not as bad as you think it is," I tell her.

"Wait!" Marjorie's eyes go huge, and I worry that if she sneezes, they'll pop right out of her head. "You don't know?"

"What?" A heebie-jeebie skitters up my legs.

"You don't even know what they've done to you! And here I am, wailing my head off, and YOU DON'T EVEN KNOW?!" She bursts into a new fit of hysterical tears.

This, incidentally, is an extremely effective way to freak

someone out. Heebie-jeebies start parachuting out of the sky and landing all over me.

"Marjorie, do you think you could just, like, slow down and maybe do a yoga pose and explain what you're talking about?" I'm begging, I know. But I figure that, no matter how bad the truth is, it can't be that bad.

The phone rings. Marjorie startles as if she's been electrified, so I get it.

"Get on Facebook," Flatso demands, before I even say hello.

"Can I borrow this?" I ask Marjorie, whose laptop is open on the kitchen table. Morris the Dog paces below, and when I reach out to scratch his ears, he skitters away. Wow. Everyone's jumpy.

"That's what I'm trying to tell you!" Marjorie screeches, and throws her arm over her eyes, as if she can't bear to watch the horror.

Her screen is already open to Facebook. I have an account, but I only check it once a day or so. It's a huge time suckhole for me, so I try to stay away. I sign in and look at my newsfeed.

"This video of a Chihuahua licking a kitten?" I ask.

"Scroll down," Flatso commands, so I do, and that's when I see it.

facebook Status update.
Someone has hacked the Freakshow's accounts.

Cuckoo
Whoops, gotta get my Prozac Prescription refilled if I wanna stay out of Crazytown now that my foster mommy's dead!!
Like · Comment · Share · about an hour ago · 👥

 | Write a comment...

Zitsy
Copper pipe makes me horny!
Like · Comment · Share · about an hour ago · 👥

 | Write a comment...

Flatso
LOLZ - Just ate my own body weight in lard! Yum, yum!
Like · Comment · Share · about an hour ago · 👥

 | Write a comment...

Eggy
Gotta study hard and steal jobs from real Americans.
Like · Comment · Share · about an hour ago · 👥

 | Write a comment...

Tebow
Help! I'm a total self-righteous douche! WWJD?
Like · Comment · Share · about an hour ago · 👥

 | Write a comment...

Brainzilla
Just a few more blow jobs at the country club until I finally have enough money for those Jimmy Choo sandals!
Like · Comment · Share · about an hour ago · 👥

 | x#!%&?+$*@#%!!!b#*!!&!!!?!

"Oh my god," I whisper. I feel like I'm going to vomit.

"I can't watch!" Marjorie screeches, and runs from the room.

"The Haters hacked us," Flatso snarls. "I didn't think they were smart enough."

I didn't think they were horrible enough. But they were. They are. This is bad.

I'm not worried about myself. I don't care if everyone thinks I'm nuts.

It's Brainzilla I'm worried about.

"Hey, Katie. It's me again. Just give me a call when you get this, okay?"

I hang up and immediately start to worry that Brainzilla's voice mail isn't working. Then I worry that my phone is defective. I pick it up and listen. Dial tone. But wait—what if she just tried to call me during that one second that I was

Tim-ber, ya tree huggers!

We got 'em so GOOOOD!

They asked for it.

holding the receiver to my ear? I click off. It still doesn't ring.

I start to dial her number again and am interrupted with a call-waiting beep. I click over.

"Did you see what those assholes did to us?" Zitsy demands.

"I know—it's totally messed up. Listen, can I call you back in a few minutes?"

"I can't get through to Brainzilla."

"Me either." My throat is thick.

"Keep trying," Zitsy says, then clicks off.

The moment I get a fresh dial tone, I call Katie again.

"Hello?" a strange voice says.

I'm so surprised that someone has picked up the phone that I actually drop the receiver and fall off my bed. Literally. I didn't even know that was possible. I haul myself onto my knees and grab the receiver.

"Oh—uh—sorry, I'm trying to reach Katie Sloane?"

"Hi, Kooks."

I stare at the number display on my phone and slowly realize that the limp voice is Brainzilla's. It sounds too exhausted, too zombielike to be my best friend. But it is. God, I wish I could just reach right through the phone wires and give her a hug. "Did you see—"

"The Yale lady friended me," Brainzilla says.

I feel like I'm falling, sliding down a deep hole. I have to lean back against the bed frame to steady myself. "What?"

Dead air on the other end of the line, and Brainzilla's words start to seep into my brain. *The Yale lady friended me*. The meaning snaps into place. "She saw it?"

I can hear Katie's breath, ragged and uneven. I wait a moment for her answer, but it never comes. Instead, I just hear the soft click of the receiver.

My best friend since preschool has just hung up on me.

She has never hung up on me before. Never. Not once.

I call back, but I get dumped straight into voice mail again. "Katie? Katie?"

But I'm shouting into a black hole, a deaf in-box. I hang up.

Even though it's useless, I can't stop myself from calling again. And again.

I leave something like fifty-seven voice mail messages. I fill that black hole until nothing more can go in it. Her voice mail is full, but I keep on calling.

From my end, it sounds like it's ringing in an empty room.

Chapter 51
EVEN SCARIER STUFF

I can't sleep. I can't get the sound of the ringing phone out of my head. Even after I hang up, it just rings on and on.

I feel this desperate need to talk to Katie. I really need to know she's okay. When she said that the Yale lady saw what the Haters posted, she sounded hollow. It was the sound a dead leaf makes when it rattles on a tree just before it falls.

I really want to go over to Brainzilla's house, but she lives all the way across town. Still—maybe I could get there on my bike. Except that it's already past nine. And it's January.

Just...
thirteen...
more
miles...

A ringing phone wakes me up. I don't know when I fell asleep, but a quick glance at the clock tells me it's almost midnight.

Here is a basic life rule: Good things never happen in the middle of the night. Well, unless you order pizza really late.

My hand hesitates over the receiver for just a moment. But the phone rings again. It almost seems louder, as if it's demanding to be answered.

Flatso starts shrieking the moment I answer. "Ohmygod, Kooks! Kooks! We have to get over to Tuality right away—I don't even know if they'll let us in, but we've got to try." She sounds like she's struggling to speak, like she's crying. "Katie's there! She's stable, but—ohmygod, Kooks—just wait there, and Zitsy will be right over—"

"What? Wait—Bev—slow down, okay? What's happening in Tuality?"

"Katie! Katie's in Tuality!"

"What's she doing in Tuality?"

"She's been admitted!" Flatso's voice rises to a scream. "Mrs. Sloane told Aunt Joan to call Mom—"

The cogs in my brain click and whir, reorganizing everything Flatso has said, trying to force it to make sense. Aunt Joan. Flatso's aunt Joan is a nurse at Tuality Community Hospital. Mrs. Sloane told her to call Flatso's mom. Katie has been admitted. I sit bolt upright, suddenly understanding everything. "What happened?" *Oh my god, it's Bloom. He went after her. He hurt her—*

Marjorie pokes her head into my room. In the darkness, her eyes are shadowed, and her pale skin is almost gray. She looks like a ghost, and I'm suddenly covered in the same creepy spiderweb feeling I had the night I found Mrs. Morris in the garage.

"Oh, Kooks," Flatso wails. She's sobbing now, crying so hard that her tears have traveled through the wires, wetting the receiver in my hand. No—wait. That doesn't make sense. *Those must be my tears*, I realize as I wait for the answer I think I already know.

"Kooks—Katie tried to kill herself."

I hear someone calling my name from far away as I run into the cold, dark night. I think the person yelling must be Marjorie. I had to push past her to get out of my room, out of the house. I feel bad, but there's no time to apologize.

I have to get to Tuality.

I have no clear plan, no awareness of anything except the desperate need to get to Katie. There are shoes on my feet, but I have no idea how they got there. I'm not wearing a coat. I am wearing my Snuggie, though. Plus I'm running, so I'm warm.

I dart across a busy street.

The honking wakes me up a little, and I remember something dim about how I'm supposed to look both ways before I cross a street. I plunge forward, past a McDonald's, a Walmart, a strip club, a check cashing place. I barely notice them as I run past. My mind can only process one thought: *Katie, Katie, Katie.*

My chest is tight, and I suck in a lungful of diesel fumes. God, I'm out of shape. My calves cramp and my thighs ache as I plod one heavy boot in front of the other. Why didn't I wear running shoes? Sweat pools under my breasts, and I feel my hair sticking to my forehead. I run on. I can't stop. I can't slow down.

Katie.

My mind never gets further than that. I feel it flex, like a fist trying to hold sand. My best friend.

A group of guys coming out of a strip club eye me. "Hey, cutie!" one of them yells. "Wanna ride?" He pumps his pelvis back and forth, and his buddies laugh.

I run on.

I pass the 7-Eleven, the Dollar Tree, a Wendy's. I must have run about three miles. Only three miles! *I'm not going to make it,* I think. *I'm not.*

A war breaks out in my mind between the You-Need-to-Rests and the If-You-Stop-Now-You'll-Never-Make-Its.

I have to keep going. Katie, Katie, Katie. I can't stop. Can't stop. Another mile. Two.

Pain stabs into my side. I stumble, then run another five steps. Run on. Finally, the You-Need-to-Rests win.

Just a minute, I tell myself. *Just a minute, then I'll get up. I'll get up and run the rest of the way.*

Katie, Katie, Katie.

There's a small patch of landscaping at the edge of a gas station. I sit down on a pile of freezing mulch and pull my Snuggie close around me. I rest there a moment, then lie back. There are no stars above me. Just glare from the gas station sign and darkness beyond. I'm tired. Bone tired.

I start to wonder if I'm going to make it. I'm not sure I can get back up.

Beep! Beep!

I hear a car roll up, and fear shoots through me because I figure it must be that group of drunken strip-club guys. But I'm out of strength. I can't even sit up. *Let me die* comes into my mind, and it's terrifying, because I've never had a thought like that before.

"Cuckoo!" someone shouts, and before I can process what's happening, strong arms scoop beneath me and I smell Flatso's familiar, flowery scent and hear her voice beside my ear.

"I've got you. I've got you," she whispers over and over as she carries me to Zitsy's car.

Zitsy cranks up the heat in the car as Flatso gently fastens me into my seat belt. "We're going to see her, Kooks," she says. "We're all going. We'll take you. Don't worry." Her voice is both soothing and firm, the exact kind of voice you want to hear after running five miles through a scary part of town at midnight. It occurs to me that if Flatso were a guy instead of a girl, she'd likely be on the football team, and she would probably be one of the most popular guys in school.

But, instead, she's a girl. The world doesn't see her strength—they only see her weight. And instead of being popular, she's one of my very best friends.

My best friends.

My best friend.

Katie, Katie, Katie.

And that's the thought that wraps itself around me as Zitsy pulls out of the gas station and drives off down the black ribbon of road toward the hospital.

I reel a moment from the rush of relief I feel when I walk into the hospital. The bright lights, the warm air. I trip toward the desk and say Brainzilla's name. "Katie," I pant, "Katherine Sloane. We're looking for her."

The nurse shakes her head. "I'm sorry—visiting hours are from eight AM to ten PM," she says.

"We can't see her?" Zitsy wails. He looks devastated by this news.

"Can you at least tell us if she's okay?" I ask.

The nurse's warm brown eyes are sympathetic. "Are you a member of the immediate family?"

"Yes." This doesn't even feel like a lie.

"I'm sorry, but I'll have to see some identification."

I hesitate. "I'm not immediate family."

The nurse sighs. "Look, I know it's really hard to have to wait. But it's important for our patients to get their rest. And I'm afraid the law forbids me from giving out any information about our patients."

"We're really worried," I say, pressing my palms against the counter. "Please?" *God, is she okay? What did she do? What did she do to herself? Will she live?*

Will she be—the same?

All I want is for one answer—one answer to one question. Anything.

"We're desperate," Zitsy says. "We're begging."

"I really wish I could," she says, and she sounds like she means it. But she doesn't give us any information. I realize that she must see people like us all the time. Wow. I would break down in five seconds. I would tell all.

"Shit!" Flatso hisses at her phone. She's texting with the speed of a concert pianist. "Aunt Joan can't even tell us how Katie is because of HIPAA regs."

"Can't she give us a hint?" I ask. "What did she do? God— what if Katie's *dying*?" I sound hysterical, and I know it, but I can't stop the thoughts: *What if she blew off part of her face with a gun? What if she took a bottle of pills and gave herself brain damage? What if she jumped—*

179

"I feel sick," Zitsy says.

"She could lose her job," Flatso says apologetically.

Screw her job! I want to scream, to grab Aunt Joan and force the information out of her. *Screw her job! Screw this hospital!* Instead, I slide down the nurses' station and lie on the green-and-navy patterned carpet. It's got an intricate, mazelike design, and makes me dizzy when I look at it too closely. I shut my eyes.

I'm not doing too well.

Zitsy sits beside me and picks up my hand. "It's okay," he says. "She'll be okay."

I take a breath. Then another. It's all I can manage. I try to pretend that I'm Eggy—someone who never cries. It would be great to have her here right now, but Zitsy and Flatso couldn't get hold of her.

Without her, I'm just too exhausted to fight the tears anymore.

I'm fine. Maybe not.

If there's anything you need, I'm right here, you poor, dear girl.

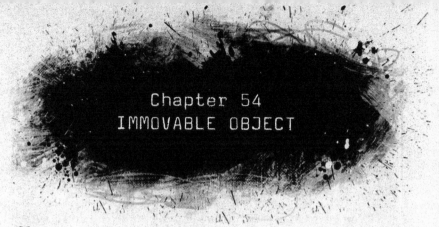

Mom, I just want to—Mom. Mom. Mom. Mom. Mom." Zitsy rolls his eyes and shakes his head at me. "Mom. Mom. Can I just say one thing? Mom. Mom." He holds the phone away from his ear, and I can hear his mother's tinny voice freaking out from across the room. "I'd better get home," Zitsy says. "I don't want my mom to hemorrhage something."

"Let's go, Kooks," Flatso says.

"I'm not leaving."

You'd better get back here right now, young man. I don't know what you think you're doing, taking your father's car at all hours of the night, but when you get home, you'll have some serious explaining to do about why you would go all the way to Tuality without even waking us up and letting us know where you are. We've been worried sick—

"Come on, Kooks," Zitsy says. "Sitting here isn't going to help anything." He looks around the slightly seedy waiting area. Orange foam is coming out of one of the chairs. Most of the magazines are torn and smeary looking. An old and slightly busted television blares in the corner.

"You guys have moms who will freak out if you don't come home. I don't."

I didn't mean for that to come out at all, but once the words are out of my mouth, I realize that they sound kind of pathetic. It's like, *Cue the violin music, people!* Ugh.

Flatso chews her lower lip, like she's stopping herself from saying something. She and Zitsy look at each other for a long time, apparently having some kind of ESP chat.

After about two minutes of meaningful glances, Flatso says, "Okay, Kooks. We'll be back first thing."

"Are you sure you're okay?" Zitsy asks.

"I'm fine," I say, trying hard to look spunky and not tragic. I lean back in my chair and look up at the television dangling in the corner. "I have my Snuggie on. I'm cozy."

Flatso gives me a hug and a quick kiss near the ear. Then she and Zitsy head out into the parking lot. As I watch them through the window, I have to fight the urge to run after them. But what good would it do? There's no point in going home. I'll just stay here…with Katie, even though she doesn't know it.

A cell phone rings, and I look around in confusion because I'm the only person in the waiting area. Until I remember that

I have a cell phone—one of those cheap in-case-of-emergency things that Mrs. Morris insisted I keep with me. I've never actually used it before.

When I pull it out of my pocket, I see that it's Mrs. Morris's number, the only one I put in the contacts. I choke on my panic, and press the talk button to say, "Oh, I'm sorry! I'm sorry for worrying you! I'll come home right away!" But before I say anything, I remember she's dead.

My mind is still reeling as I press the phone to my ear. "Cuckoo?" Marjorie is saying. "Kooks? Are you there?"

"Marjorie?" My voice is a hoarse whisper, scratchy as sandpaper.

"Oh, I'm so glad I reached you! Are you okay? Are you coming home?"

"I'm at the hospital in Tuality—"

"The *hospital*?"

There's fear in her voice, and it leaves me weak with surprise. I hadn't realized that she cared about me—that she would want to know where I was and whether I was all right. I hadn't thought of her at all. But she saw me rush out of the house in the middle of the night—she must have been worried.

"I'm okay, I'm okay. It's Katie. She's—hurt. And they won't let me see her and…" My voice starts to quaver, and I have to count ceiling tiles until I feel somewhat normal again. "Anyway, I don't think I can leave. I don't *want* to leave until I know she's okay."

The line is quiet, and in the space of the silence, I realize something. Even though I've been living with Marjorie, I've been treating her the way you treat a wobbly desk. Like something that isn't ideal, but is okay for now. But Marjorie isn't a desk; she's a person. She's Mrs. Morris's daughter.

I feel bad for treating her like furniture.

"I understand," Marjorie says finally. And it really sounds like she does.

Marjorie may be a flake, but she's a flake who seems to actually get me. I don't know what that means, but it's true.

I'm staring blankly at the television screen in the hospital waiting room when I hear someone sit down beside me.

"He isn't guilty," Marjorie whispers, jutting her chin at the TV. "It's the blond prep-school teen who witnessed the crime."

I click off the television. We're the only two people in the waiting room, so nobody protests. In the sudden quiet, I hear the walls humming around me, full of the sounds of machines and people breathing in rooms beyond.

"Are you here to keep me company?" I ask. "Or to take me home?"

"I'm here to convince you that you need a hamburger," she says. Marjorie spreads the fabric of her Indian skirt over the torn chair cushion, hiding its orange foam guts.

"I don't want to leave."

"I know, but you can't get in to see her until eight, anyway. We'll just hit the drive-through and come right back." Marjorie sees me hesitate, and adds, "You have to come with me! I'm starving, but those drive-through intercoms freak me out. Don't make me go alone. Please?"

Then she gently takes my hand and tugs on it until I follow her to the door. I'm too numb to put up much of a fight.

Marjorie's car is a vintage Buick and smells like an old man. But it's still warm from her trip out to find me, and it's snug as we drive around looking for burger places. I tuck the Snuggie I'm wearing under my thighs.

"I always love driving around at night, don't you?" Marjorie says. We pass a streetlight, and it illuminates her face, then plunges her into darkness again.

"I don't really do it much." A country-western song mumbles from the radio. I can't make out the words to the song, but it's comforting, somehow.

"Mom and I used to drive at night all the time. Especially in the winter. We'd head out and look at people's Christmas lights. In summer, we'd drive around with the windows open, let the

Just toss the fries out the window so I don't have to Stop!

DiE ThrU

JACK'S VALUE MENU
BLOOD BURGER
French fingers
EYE SCREAM
Fried Legs
Grilled Tongue
SNAKES

breeze blow over us." Marjorie is smiling as she says this. It's sweet to imagine her and Mrs. Morris out for a drive.

"She always supported me," Marjorie says. "Even when I wasn't a very good daughter, she always acted like I put the stars in the sky. I was so lucky."

"You were," I agree. We both were.

"She never told me to get a real job or to give up on my screenplay," Marjorie goes on. "She believed in me. Even when I had doubts, she always believed."

Marjorie is humming to herself as she drives, and I realize that she's not just a crazy flake. She's a person following her dream. When you look at it in a certain light, she's incredibly brave.

I lean my head against the glass and look out the window. We're passing a strip mall, like a million others, but the lights look pretty to me, glowing in the darkness like that. It's a strange, beautiful world, but I don't think I understand it very well.

Katie seemed perfect.

Marjorie seemed flaky.

I'm starting to think I'm not such a good judge of whether or not people have it together.

Kooks." Marjorie shakes my shoulder gently. "Kooks, wake up."

"Ohmygod—what time is it?" After a late-night burger and fries, I've fallen asleep in the waiting room. Damned cozy Snuggie! Damned comfy chair!

"Seven fifty-five. Visiting hours start at eight. I knew you didn't want to be late."

I catch sight of our shadowy reflections in the long windows across the room. Marjorie's hair is as wild as usual, and mine is sticking up straight on one side and plastered to my head on the other. That, combined with my bright red Snuggie (matted with wood chips and sporting a mustard stain from my midnight burger), makes me look like something you'd find in a Dumpster the day after Christmas. I try to fluff/smooth my hair, but give up after a few seconds. Katie isn't going to notice. She cares about her own clothes, but not anyone else's.

"Do you want me to stay?" Marjorie asks. "I can wait for you."

I give her a little hug, and she pats my back with her small, nervous hands. "Zitsy will take me home," I tell her. "You go get some sleep. It's almost your bedtime, anyway."

Marjorie's mouth twitches a half laugh, and she rakes her long, elegant fingers through her bird's-nest hair. "If you need me, call me. I'll keep the phone by my pillow."

There's a new nurse on duty, and she looks up Brainzilla's room number, then directs me to the elevator. I'm so impatient that I try to calm myself by counting. I do that sometimes. It's kind of Zen. Anyway, I'm muttering "one hundred and forty-four" by the time I finally find Brainzilla's room. She's mostly asleep when I tiptoe in. She looks pale and drained under the bright hospital lights.

I'm so relieved to see her that my eyes start leaking like mad, just pouring water down my face. I don't make any noise, though. I don't want to completely wake her up.

There's a hideous pink chair beside her bed, and I sit in it and watch her sleep. Her face isn't blown off. No limbs seem to be missing—no bruises at the neck, no slashes on the arms. She must have taken pills. I sit there, staring and thinking, for seventeen minutes before her breath catches and her eyes snap open. She sits straight up.

What time is it? Am I late for school?

She looks around the room frantically, as if she has no idea where she is. Then her eyes land on me.

"Hi, Katie," I say softly.

And then her face sort of collapses on itself and she falls back against the rumpled pillow.

Brainzilla is silent a long time, staring up at the ceiling. "I'm in a hospital," she says.

"Yes."

"And my mother isn't here."

Beyond the door, the floor is waking up. An orderly passes by with a cart. Two doctors are chatting at the nurses' station. "She was here when they admitted you. Visiting hours just started. I'm sure she'll be here soon."

My best friend doesn't look at me. She just keeps her eyes trained on the ceiling tiles. "Dad is probably just getting home from his shift. Mom will have to open the day care in a few minutes. She can't close down—the parents are counting on her. If they don't have day care, they can't work, and if they can't work, they get fired." Machinery hums all around us. "I'm sure she'll come by afterward."

"Your mom loves you."

"I know that. It's just life, you know? If she shuts the day care—even for a day—the families will go somewhere else. Then we'll all suffer. I don't even know how she's going to pay for this." She gestures to the hideous hospital room. "God, I wish I'd thought of that."

"The government—"

"They still make you pay part of it." Katie wraps the white sheet around her hand. "The Yale lady saw what they wrote, Kooks."

"But it wasn't true."

"She doesn't know that." Her blue eyes lock on mine.

"Katie, the world won't end if you don't get into Yale."

"I don't want my parents' life."

"There are a thousand ways to have a different life. A million! Yale is just one. Just *one*."

Brainzilla looks out the window. She's in a semiprivate room, but there's nobody in the other bed, so she has it all to herself. Outside, the sky is pale blue, and the sun shines on the icy white below, making the trees sparkle.

"I love you, Kooks," she says. "I even love that you're wearing the Snuggie I gave you."

I reach for her hand. Her elegant manicured fingers intertwine with my ragged ones. "I love you, too," I tell her.

Then we settle into the kind of silence that you can only share with a best friend.

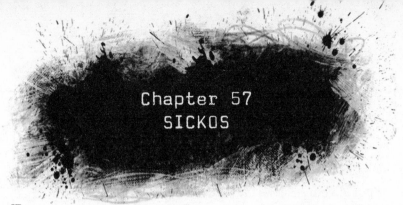

Chapter 57
SICKOS

Flatso pokes her head in, takes one look at me and Brainzilla, and yells, "She's sitting up!" over her shoulder.

"She is?" Eggy asks, pushing her way through the doorframe. Her cheeks are pink from the cold, and she beams when she sees Brainzilla. "You're alive!"

Flatso, Zitsy, and Eggy pile onto Katie's bed, hugging her and laughing. Tebow hovers awkwardly nearby, his eyes closed and his hand over his heart. I wonder if he's praying, giving a little shout-out to the Lord or Baby Jesus for taking care of Brainzilla. It occurs to me that maybe I should say thank you, too.

Finally, Tebow steps forward and plants a delicate kiss on Brainzilla's forehead. His lips linger a moment, and I see him breathe in once, twice. I can tell he's just as relieved as I am.

"Who needs a doughnut?" Flatso asks, opening a huge box.

Zitsy reaches for three, and suddenly the hospital room is like a party. Eggy has brought along her trumpet, and she plays a very bouncy

Thank you, God, or Buddha, or Jesus, or Allah, or the Great Universe, or science, or whatever. Thank you for saving my best friend. Thank you.

version of "When the Saints Go Marching In."

Brainzilla doesn't have a doughnut, but she smiles and even manages to laugh when Zitsy gets a pink sprinkle stuck on the end of his nose. It's kind of amazing how there can still be room in your heart to laugh, even when something really scary and sad has happened.

"I'd like to make an announcement," Zitsy says, reaching into his pocket. "I have something I'd like to give you." He holds out a fist and lets it hover there—right over Brainzilla's lap for a dramatic moment. Then he uncurls his fingers, revealing a beautiful gold filigree ring. At the center is a large emerald-cut ruby.

Brainzilla creates a new vowel between *O* and *U*. She's so shocked that she doesn't even reach for it.

Eggy purses her lips. "Are you proposing to Brainzilla, Zitsy?"

"Where did you get that?" I ask.

"I found it in a clogged pipe," he admits. "The lady who owned the house said it wasn't hers, so I reported it to the police, but they just told me to keep it. Which is fair, I think, because I'm the one who dug it out of the sewage."

Brainzilla blinks a little bit, like she isn't sure whether to take it. But—after a minute— she takes the ring and puts it on. She never could resist anything sparkly.

"It's beautiful," she breathes.

"When you wear it, you should remember how much we all care about you," Zitsy says.

"I'll remember all the crap I have to put up with," Brainzilla shoots back.

Which reminds me of a song.

"When the night has come," I sing, "and the land is dark…" I feel everyone staring at me, and my voice trails off.

Note to self: Bursting into song does not go unnoticed.

I don't know what made me start spewing that song. "Stand by Me" was one of Mrs. Morris's favorites. It just popped into my head while I was standing here, feeling the love. Now I just feel my ears burning with embarrassment.

"Go on, Kooks," Tebow says gently. Then he starts the next line, "And the moon…" He has a nice voice—a strong tenor. I hesitate a moment, looking at my friends.

And then Eggy puts her trumpet to her lips and plays along. Soon, the room is filled with our voices as we all join in.

We only get to sing for a few minutes before a nurse comes and tells us to shut up. But still, those moments are beautiful.

Beautiful.

I can't explain why, but this is exactly what we all needed— just to be together.

We really are going to be okay.

All of us.

Chapter 58
SCHOOL DAZE

The next morning, I'm still feeling trashed. I skipped school to stay at the hospital with Brainzilla yesterday. But they're releasing her today, and I can't just avoid the world forever.

In homeroom, I feel like I'm walking a tightrope—one wrong step could send me plunging toward the hard ground. The school announcements do their fifteen minutes of blahblah, so I put my head down on my desk and close my eyes. The minute I do that, though, I hear the phone ringing in my mind—the same phone that kept ringing and ringing the night I tried to get in touch with Katie. And then something really scary happens.

I can't find Laurence anywhere. I can't remember his face. I can't hear his voice—the phone in my brain is too loud.

And that's the step—the step off the tightrope.

I start crying. Bawling, really. The class goes silent, and all the kids around me avert their eyes. I feel Flatso's hand on my shoulder, and Zitsy murmurs, "Oh, Kooks, oh, Kooks." But I can hardly hear him. All I hear is that goddamn phone.

I keep on crying when the bell rings, and for the first eight minutes of first period. I'm finally starting to pull it together, take shaky breaths and all that, and then—surprise, surprise,

Ms. Alter shows up at the door and beckons me down the hall to Ms. Kellerman's office.

When I walk in, she's sitting in her chair. She's got the same look on her face that supervillains always wear when they capture James Bond. It's that moment when they feel like their plan is really coming together.

This isn't really a look that you want on your psychologist.

"Hello, Margaret," she says, gesturing for me to have a seat. "I've heard what occurred two days ago. I'm very sorry."

"Okay," I say, because I can't bear to say thank you.

"I have been informed that you have not been handling the situation well." Ms. Kellerman starts rooting through her pencil cup, as if she's talking to the pens, maybe hoping to get their advice. "I fear this represents a real crisis in your case."

"I wouldn't call it a crisis."

She selects a pen, then looks up at me—finally meeting my eye. "Then what would you call it?"

"Appropriate sadness?"

"Do you think that crying in homeroom is appropriate?"

"Not really."

"And skipping school yesterday—was that appropriate? The hospital in Tuality informs me that you spent the night in the waiting room. That you refused to go home. Is that appropriate?"

A hot, angry tear leaks from my right eye. This is enough to convince Ms. Kellerman that I'm going over the edge.

"Margaret, you need to accept the fact that you are mentally ill. You've already been hospitalized once, and I think you should consider that option once more." She starts signing some paperwork, which sends a creepy feeling all over me. "I'm writing out a recommendation—"

"What?" The word bursts from my mouth like a scream.

"Margaret, I'm concerned that you might be a danger to yoursel—"

Danger! Danger? I grab her pencil cup and dump the writing implements on the floor. Then I stomp on them.

It feels really good to hear those pens and pencils crunch under the soles of my Uggs.

Ms. Kellerman is totally speechless, and I'm not going to lie: I feel really good for wiping that supervillain grin off her face. In fact, I feel better than I have in three days.

"Wow, Ms. Kellerman," I say, "I think you've cured me. Thanks."

And then—before she can think of anything to say or even stand up to stop me—I walk right out the door.

Crisis!
Crossroads!
Slippery slope!
Danger to yourself!
Meds!
Hospitalization!

Actually, none of that is as helpful as Pen-crunching.

Kooks!" Marjorie meets me at the front door the minute I get home from school. "What happened?" Her nervous little hands flutter to her throat.

"Did they call you?" I ask, but a moment later, I look past her and get my answer. Mr. Tenant Goldborough is sitting on our couch in the living room. Beside him stands Billy, one of the attendants from St. Augustine Hospital.

"Margaret, I'm afraid I have some bad news," Mr. Goldborough says.

"Hi, Billy," I say. "It's been a while." Billy isn't a bad guy. He's got broad features and the flat expression of someone who doesn't ask a lot of questions, which is probably what makes him good at his job.

He sighs and looks at the paperwork in Mr. Goldborough's hand. "I'm sorry, Maggie."

I shrug. It looks like Ms. Kellerman got everyone's attention. I guess I shouldn't have attacked her pencil cup like that. My insides feel heavy—like I just ate a giant block of cheese, or concrete, or something. Ms. Kellerman claims to be so worried about my fragile psyche. Did it ever occur to her that sending people off to the loony bin is the kind of thing that makes them crazy?

But I don't pitch a fit. I don't even argue. I just let Billy put a warm hand on my elbow and guide me out the door.

"Oh, Kooks!" Marjorie's hands have sunk into her hair.

"I'll be back," I tell her, and try to smile. "Don't worry. Everything's going to be okay."

"You sound like my mother," Marjorie calls after me as we step outside into the steady rain.

I don't know if it's true, but I cling to that compliment like a gold coin. I want to put it in my pocket and examine it later. If I could be like Mrs. Morris—even a little bit—
then I know I'll get through this.

Why do you think you were crying in class?" Dr. Marcuse asks me.

I'm sitting in her office across from a funky green felt wall hanging. It's a thousand shades of green, like a forest, and I love looking at it. It's funny—I don't like the fact that Ms. Kellerman *sent* me here, but I don't mind actually *being* here. "I was crying because I was sad," I tell Dr. Marcuse. "Because my best friend nearly died."

Dr. Marcuse takes off her glasses and polishes them with a handkerchief. I love that she has a handkerchief. It's so old-fashioned and elegant. "Can you think of a more appropriate response?"

"Not really."

"Neither can I," Dr. Marcuse says, perching her glasses back on her nose. "Do you have any idea how the school administration expected you to react? What they would consider appropriate?"

"Increased study time, maybe?"

Dr. Marcuse laughs softly, like a cat's purr. "No doubt that was their hope."

"Sometimes I just feel like I'm going to be sad forever," I say. "Like my blue period is going to turn into my blue life, and I'll just be a loser who cries nonstop and feels sorry for herself."

"How much do you believe that? One hundred percent?"

"Thirty, maybe. Thirty-five? Thirty-three. No. Twenty-eight." I can't quite come up with the perfect number, but it's in that range.

"So—less than half. You don't really believe it, in other words. A small part of you thinks it, but you don't really believe it."

"Yeah."

"Is there anything that makes you happy now?"

"Well, Katie's okay," I say.

"Yes, that's good."

I think a moment. "And I have my other friends. And Marjorie—she's been really sweet to me. I'm starting to see how we could be…" I shrug, unsure what to say. *Friends? Foster relatives?* "We could really get along."

Dr. Marcuse nods. "Good."

I think about Morris the Dog. And Laurence, and all the books at the library. And all those happy things make me start to feel a little bit better.

I can even imagine a day when I'm just happy and nothing else.

I'm not there yet. The hospital and Mrs. Morris and my mom and everything—it's all still too raw. But someday.

"You have a right to be sad, Maggie. You're fine. Sadness is not a mental illness."

I look back up at the leafy wall hanging. The forest. Even trees go though sad times. But then they burst back to life. *That will be me*, I tell myself.

That will be me.

Go home. You're better than half the doctors in here. I'm serious.

Oh, and please don't put that in your diary — or at least change my name if you do.

Finally, Monday comes around. It's Brainzilla's first day
back from the hospital. It's my first day back from the mental
hospital. We've barely set foot in homeroom before we get
called to Mr. Tool's office.

Those guys really know how to give a girl some space. Like,
thismuch.

The rest of the Freakshow is already sitting in Mr. Tool's
office when we arrive. Flatso is wearing tons of navy eye
shadow, which gives her a menacing, glowering look. Everyone
else seems blank, except for Zitsy, who is staring at Mr. Tool as
if he's a cliff he might fall off. We're definitely not at our best,
and being called in to see Mr. Tool isn't making things better.

"What's up?" I ask.

"Chicken butt!" Zitsy says involuntarily. He clamps a hand
over his mouth as nobody laughs.

Mr. Tool taps his fingers against his desk impatiently, then
snaps up a paper lying there. "What do you know about this?"
he asks, brandishing one of our Rally for Reason fliers.

"Um…that we're pro-reason?" I say, looking at the others.

"I made that," Eggy announces. "We wanted to do
something positive for the school."

"Well, I'm afraid that this event has been canceled," Mr. Tool announces. "You can't simply schedule an event on school grounds without the proper permission and clearance."

For a moment, we all just stare at one another.

"How do we get the proper permission and clearance?" Zitsy asks.

Mr. Tool gives him a narrow-eyed smile. "You can submit an application to my office."

"Okay." Tebow stands up, as if the matter is settled. "We'll do that."

"I'm afraid your application has been denied," Mr. Tool says.

Tebow—bless his sweet, innocent self—looks confused. "How can it be denied if we haven't submitted it yet?"

Mr. Tool throws our flyer in the trash. "That's how. This event is not happening. Not this weekend. Not next weekend. Not in my lifetime." He shoots a look at me.

"Why?" I ask. The word dribbles from my lips like a coffee spilling from the edge of a chipped mug.

"Because you can't handle it." Mr. Tool's voice isn't mean, but his words stab through me, anyway. I feel all eyes dart to Brainzilla, who is studying the carpet, unmoving in that comfortable chair of his. It takes all my energy not to lunge across Mr. Tool's desk and take a swipe at him. What's he trying to do—make Katie take another bottle of pills?

I hear the door open and turn to see Tebow's back as he leaves the office. Eggy is next, and then the rest of us rise and file out.

Our event is banned.

Operation Happiness is over.

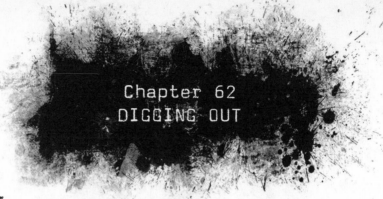

Chapter 62
DIGGING OUT

The back stairwell is claustrophobic and a really sickly shade of green. Also, the faint smell of barf seems to linger in the corner closest to the door, and it's always about fifteen degrees hotter than the rest of the school. The windows here are the industrial kind threaded through with slim wire, and someone has used one as a canvas on which to scratch a lovely image of an angry penis.

I usually avoid the back stairwell because it makes me feel like I'm stuck in the Grinch's pocket. Then again, everyone else avoids it, too. So it's a good place to come if you want to be alone.

Which I do.

I can't believe our Rally for Reason has been banned. The school doesn't want *reason*. Literally. It's not even a *metaphor*.

The door pops open, and I turn away, not wanting to make eye contact with whoever has chosen to walk through this wasteland.

"You're gonna die," Digger Whitlock announces.

"I know that, Digger." I look up at him. He's blinking at the angry penis, like he can't make sense of it. "Why do you keep reminding me?"

Digger sits down beside me. His fat, square fingers reach out to touch the vomit-green paint, and when he moves, his clothes

PLATO
((COURAGE IS
KNOWING WHAT
NOT TO FEAR))

SOCRATES
((THE ONLY THING
I TRULY KNOW...
IS THAT I KNOW
NOTHING))

ARISTOTLE
((HAPPINESS DEPENDS
UPON OURSELVES))

release the faint smell of wood smoke. He traces a circle, keeping his eyes on the wall. "People need reminding." His voice is slow, almost mechanical. "If everyone remembers that they're going to die, then maybe they'll remember to live." His eyes slide across the floor. "My brother didn't get a chance to live, Maggie. Andy never even thought about it."

"I know. I'm sorry."

Digger's eyes lift to meet mine. All this time, I've heard Digger telling us that we were going to die, but I've never bothered to wonder what he meant by it. I just thought he was borderline nuts, and trying to scare us. And as I meet his soft brown gaze, I see something I didn't expect: reason.

It's like he and I are having our own mini rally right here, in the Grinch's pocket.

"You're right," I tell Digger. "I am going to die. We all are. But not today."

"Not today," he agrees.

I look up at the glass, past the iron threads and the angry penis, and realize that outside, the sky is perfectly blue. I've been looking at the window instead of the sky.

"DON'T
FORGET TO
LIVE
—DIGGER
WHITLOCK"

He's a Philosopher— who knew?

We can't give up on the rally. I can't. I won't.

It's time to call an emergency meeting of the Freakshow.

THE FREAKSHOW THINK TANK!

Chapter 63
SCREAM OUT

YEEEEAAHH!

AIEEEEE!

STOMP!   STOMP!   STOMP!

But we still can't hold it on campus. They'll ban us again.

Flatso-stotle

Then we'll hold it off campus. On the town green.

Egg-fuscious

SCREAM OUT

SATURDAY
Nothing will stop us!

Scream, shout, let it all out!
Saturday noon
Town green

Chapter 64
BEYOND OUR WILDEST DREAMS

Here is the thing about Facebook: Its power can be used for evil…but can also be used for good. So we harness its power and invite everyone to the Scream Out. We send e-mails and put flyers up around town. We've planned the Scream Out for Saturday, which is only two days away. That means turnout will be small. But, in a way, the fact that we don't have much time is an advantage—there's less time for the school to find out, and less time for us to come to our senses and back out.

Flatso's mom works for the mayor's office, so she gets us a permit for the town green. Eggy knows a bunch of musicians, and a local band called Flying Squirrel says we can borrow their microphones and speakers. Zitsy's dad gets some carpenter friends to volunteer to build us a stage. Tebow even persuades the local bakery to donate a bunch of cookies. What else do you need to do to organize a bunch of people to get together and scream? I mean, I could pretty much do that in my living room with zero planning whatsoever.

On Saturday, Tebow shows up about an hour before the Scream Out to pick me up. He seems a little nervous as we drive downtown in his dad's old car, but I'm not. Even if it's just the Freakshow, I'm ready to scream and eat cookies.

There's a light dusting of snow on the ground, but the air is warm, which has made the day misty and gray. It softens the edges of the buildings and trees beyond the car window and makes me feel as if I'm drifting through a cloud.

The traffic slows as we near downtown, and Tebow frowns as we inch forward. "Something's going on," he says. "There are a ton of cars."

I lean forward to peer through the window. "A concert, or something?" I ask. "This is going to mess up the rally."

"We should've checked the town calendar." He turns down a side street, but cars are parked on either side. We end up parking six blocks away and walking toward the town green. I feel the sun slanting in toward us, and I wonder if some of the mist will burn off and the snow will melt.

As we get closer, we notice a lot of familiar faces on foot. "Hey, man," Tommy Marinachi says.

"Where you headed?" Tebow asks, pounding Tommy's fist and nodding at a couple of other guys from the football team.

"Scream Out," Tommy replies, and my surprise hasn't even had time to wear off before we turn a corner and come to the town green, which is thronged. I mean THRONGED. Yes—it's so crowded that I need an SAT word to describe it.

Horns are blaring, and traffic is totally messed up, and I see Zitsy standing at the microphone, looking joyful. The crowd is even better than I had dreamed it—all the Nations are represented. It's like the High School UN. Even the Haters are there.

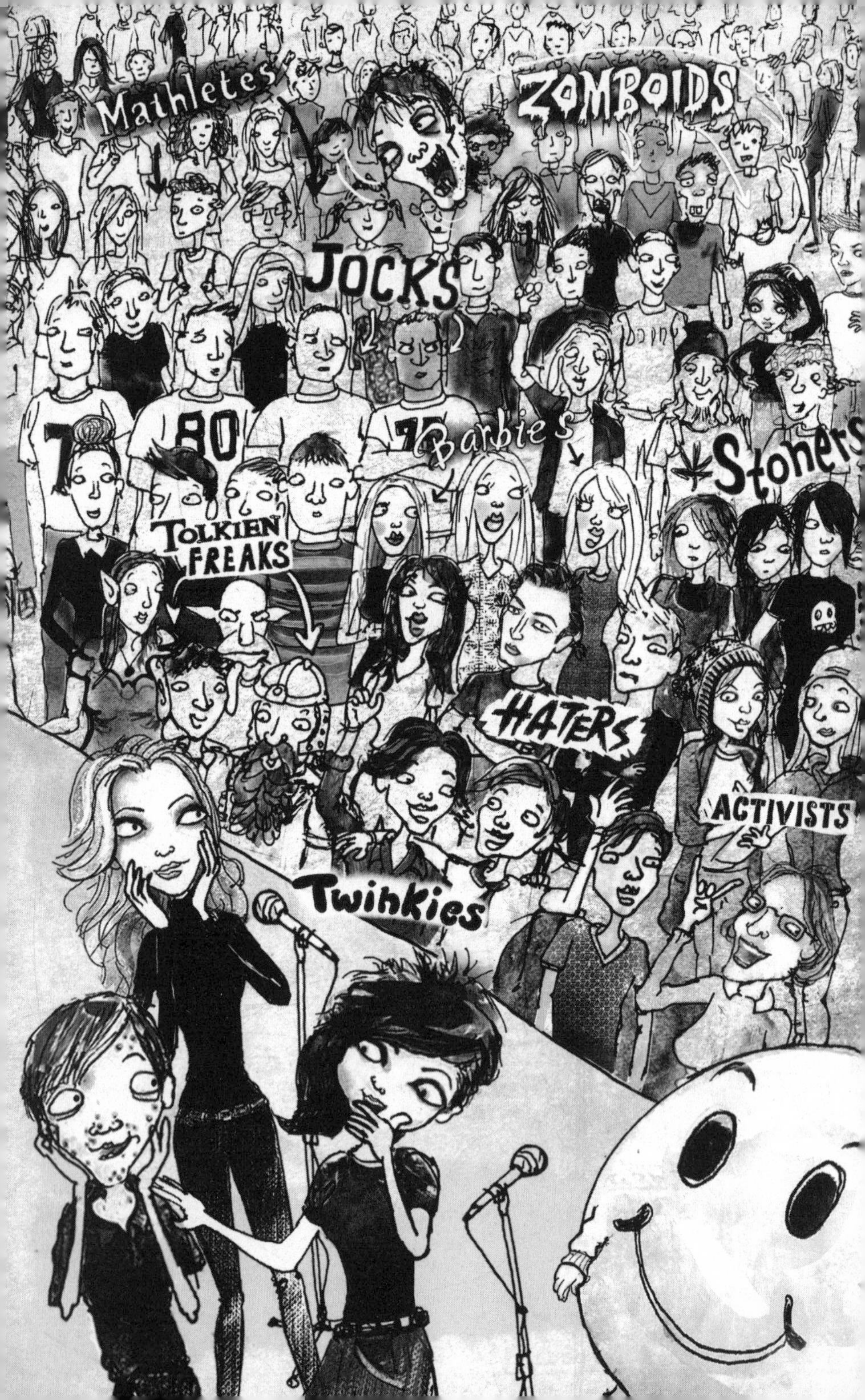
Mathletes
ZOMBOIDS
JOCKS
80
Barbies
Stoners
TOLKIEN FREAKS
HATERS
ACTIVISTS
Twinkies

"Was anyone expecting this many people?" I ask Brainzilla.

"Dude, we are going to have a serious cookie shortage." Zitsy chews a fingernail, then spits it out. Disgusting, but I totally understand the sentiment.

"Are these guys expecting a speech or something?" Flatso asks. "Or celebrities? Why are they here?"

"I didn't really prepare anything." Brainzilla is holding her hand over the microphone. "I didn't think more than twenty people would come."

I put my hand on her shoulder, and say the first true thing that occurs to me. "You can handle it," I tell her.

She heaves a deep breath. "Okay." Brainzilla steps to the front of the stage, and Zitsy hands her the mic. I see her hand shaking, but her voice is solid as she says, "Are you ready to scream?"

A few people shout, "Yeah," and I wonder if they only just realized that we were the ones who organized this event. *Please don't leave*, I think, but nobody does.

"I said, ARE YOU READY TO SCREAM?!" Brainzilla shouts into the microphone.

And this time, the response is deafening.

All at once, everyone yells, "YEAH!"

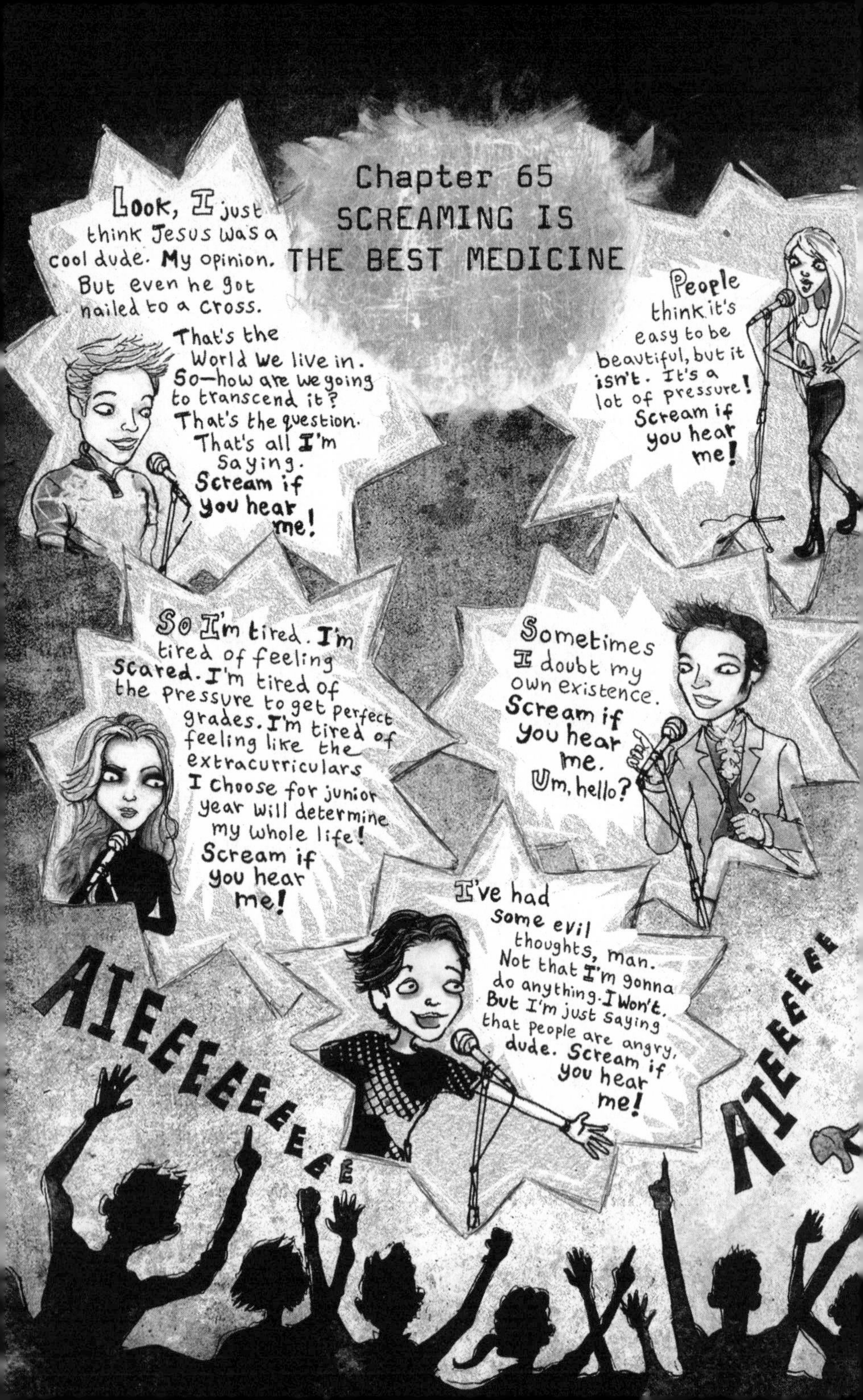
Chapter 65
SCREAMING IS THE BEST MEDICINE
Look, I just think Jesus was a cool dude. My opinion. But even he got nailed to a cross. That's the world we live in. So—how are we going to transcend it? That's the question. That's all I'm saying. Scream if you hear me!
People think it's easy to be beautiful, but it isn't. It's a lot of pressure! Scream if you hear me!
So I'm tired. I'm tired of feeling scared. I'm tired of the pressure to get perfect grades. I'm tired of feeling like the extracurriculars I choose for junior year will determine my whole life! Scream if you hear me!
Sometimes I doubt my own existence. Scream if you hear me. Um, hello?
I've had some evil thoughts, man. Not that I'm gonna do anything. I won't. But I'm just saying that people are angry, dude. Scream if you hear me!
AIEEEEEEEEEE
AIEEEEEE

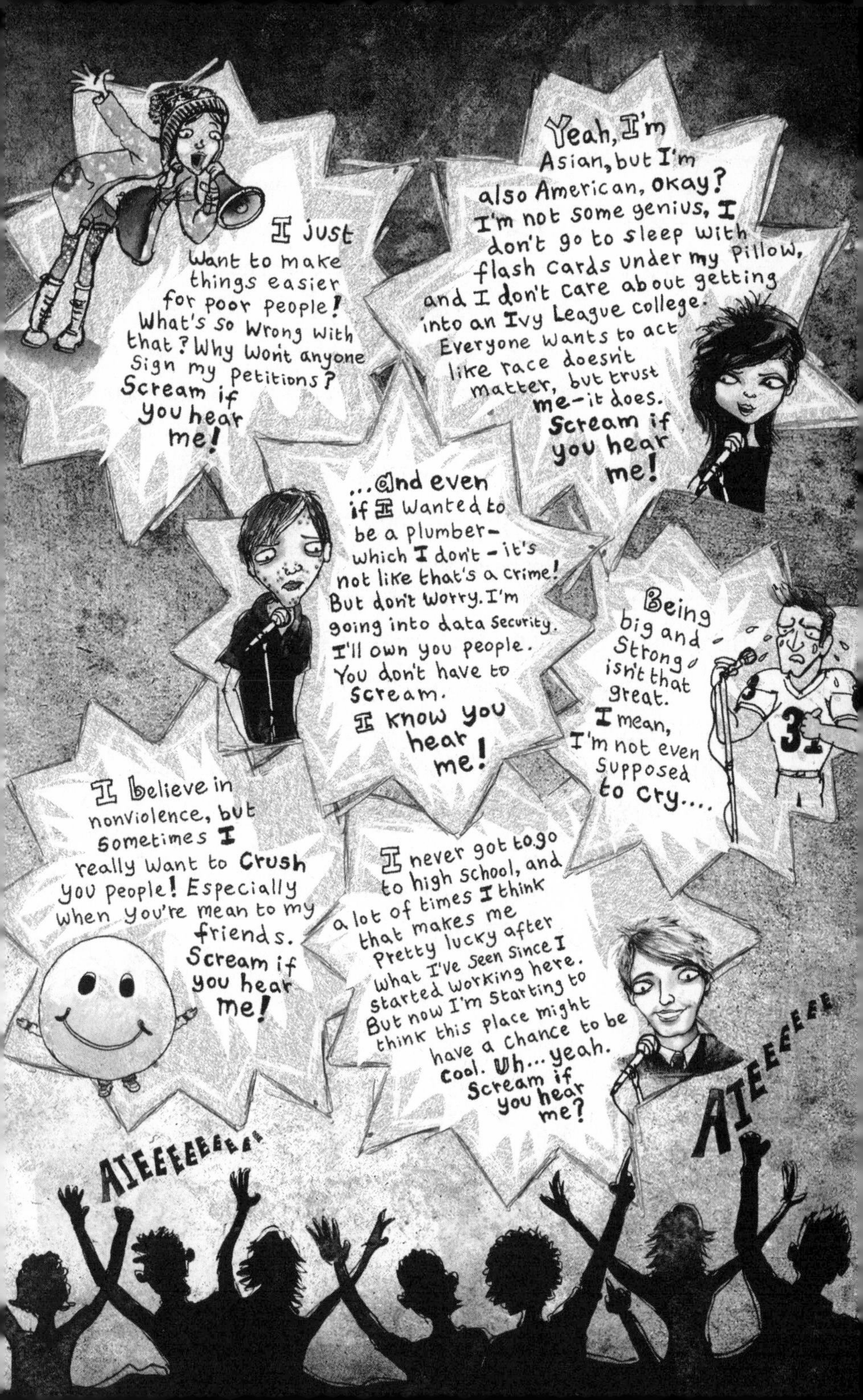
I just want to make things easier for poor people! What's so wrong with that? Why won't anyone sign my petitions? Scream if you hear me!
Yeah, I'm Asian, but I'm also American, okay? I'm not some genius, I don't go to sleep with flash cards under my pillow, and I don't care about getting into an Ivy League college. Everyone wants to act like race doesn't matter, but trust me—it does. Scream if you hear me!
...and even if I wanted to be a plumber—which I don't—it's not like that's a crime! But don't worry. I'm going into data security. I'll own you people. You don't have to scream. I know you hear me!
Being big and strong isn't that great. I mean, I'm not even supposed to cry....
I believe in nonviolence, but sometimes I really want to crush you people! Especially when you're mean to my friends. Scream if you hear me!
I never got to go to high school, and a lot of times I think that makes me pretty lucky after what I've seen since I started working here. But now I'm starting to think this place might have a chance to be cool. Uh... yeah. Scream if you hear me?
AIEEEEEEEEE
AIEEEEEEEE

One by one, familiar faces step up to the mic. And as they speak, they become real people to me.

The fog has burned off, and the sun is out. The day is warming up, and I have to take off my hat to keep my brain from melting. I've never listened so hard for so long in my life, and I start yawning uncontrollably. But I don't want to go home.

A Twinkie I don't know—Jim? Jeff?—hands me half a chocolate chip cookie, and I sit down on the grass. The cookie crumbles as I take a bite, sinking my teeth into a dense chunk of dark chocolate. Instantly, I feel more awake, and I realize that Zitsy was right about the importance of snacks.

I'm surrounded by kids who are planted on the grass, listening as everyone sounds his or her own barbaric yawp over the green. Some people cry. One girl even gets up there and sings an Indigo Girls song. And everyone listens.

We just listen.

It's like group therapy for the whole school. With cookies. And it's mostly very peaceful.

Chapter 66
MY NAME IS MARGARET,
OR MAGGIE, IF YOU LIKE

Go ahead, Kooks," Flatso says as she hands me the microphone. "Tell them how it is."

I've been standing on the grass and listening for about an hour, and I somehow drifted into the speaker's line. I didn't mean to. Well, I don't think I meant to.

Did I mean to?

Tebow notices my hesitation, and says, "You don't have to," in this really gentle way that kind of makes me want to hug him and burst into tears at the same time.

I nod and hand the microphone back to Flatso, but I also walk out to the center of the stage, so I guess my brain and body are still not quite in synch. I'm a little worried about what might happen next.

"Can everyone hear me?" I ask.

"Yes," the crowd choruses. "Louder!" someone shouts from the back.

"Um, hi. Hello. I'm, uh—I'm—" What's my name? I think. For some reason, I don't want to say, *I'm Cuckoo.*

I look out at the crowd. Nobody shouts anything. Nobody boos. And then my eyes light upon Winnie. He's standing at the center of the crowd, but the sunlight is shining on his hair and it's like everyone else melts away. He's the only person I can see, and he's smiling. I remember him telling me that I could talk to him, if I ever needed to.

Just pretend you're talking to Winnie, I tell myself.

"I'm Margaret," I say. "Maggie. And I want to thank everyone for showing up today. We"—I look over at the Freakshow—"we really didn't expect it."

And then someone in the crowd shouts, "We love you, Maggie!" A few people clap. Not even my friends—just people.

"I love you, too," I say. My eyes seek out Winnie, and he nods. "And I know that sounds crazy, but it's true. Look, I've lost a lot this year. My mom left. I had to go to a mental hospital for a while. My foster mother died. My friend…got sick. And that was really, really terrifying. For a while, I was barely holding on. But Brainzilla—Katie—had this idea that we should try to make other people happy. That it would make us feel better to help others. So this whole year, my friends and I have been trying to bring the Nations together. Brainzilla, Zitsy, Flatso, Tebow, Eggy—all of us—we just had this cool idea that maybe school didn't have to suck," I say.

The sun is really getting hot now, and I feel my tongue drying out. Zitsy hands me his water bottle. I take a grateful swig.

"Anyway, we came up with this idea—this Operation Happiness. And we tried to bring everyone a little closer, you know? And it was a complete fail on every level. For months, it was fail after fail." I look out over the crowd, and I can actually feel the energy. I can feel everyone listening, straining to understand. And just that—just everyone listening—makes me feel light and happy, like I'm a balloon that might just sail away over the trees and into the clouds.

"We failed on every level," I repeat, my voice stronger, "until today. And I just have to say this: I love all of you! Sorry if that sounds cheesy, but I really do. I love everything we share. Now that people are being brave enough to speak out, and brave enough to listen, I can see just how much we have in common. When you stop and think about it—it's a lot. Nobody here has it easy. Nobody. There's a lot more that binds us together than there is that drives us apart."

I step back. I forget to say, "Scream if you can hear me," but it's okay. We don't all have to scream. Some of us can whisper.

Winnie waves to me, and I wave back.

Are people supposed to cry at rallies? Not really sure, but lots of kids are doing it. Even one of the guy gym teachers is boo-hooing up a storm. So, if we are gauging the success by the level of tears, I guess this rally is a triumph.

It's at least a start.

No," Tebow says suddenly, putting up a hand to block the next speaker. Flatso is still holding the microphone, like she can't decide whether to hand it over.

It's Bloom.

"Why not?" he demands.

Brainzilla folds her arms across her chest. "You aren't welcome here."

I hear a murmur from the crowd, and my stomach goes funny. Bloom is glowering, his eyes shifting and snakelike, and I'm amazed that I ever thought he was handsome.

But he's here, at the rally. And isn't the point of the rally that we're giving everyone a chance to speak?

"Zilla," I murmur, "come on."

She shoots me a warning look, like she knows what I'm going to say. But I say it anyway. "He deserves a chance. Everyone deserves a chance."

Brainzilla throws her hands in the air. "Fine," she snaps. Then she draws a deep breath in and says, "Okay." A little more softly, like she really means it.

I nod at Flatso, who hands over the mic, and Bloom steps to the center of the stage. He clears his throat. "Listen, I just wanted to say I'm sorry," he says, and I'm once again back in my balloon, floating and happy. We did it! We really did it! We have reached Marty Bloom!

He looks back over his shoulder and catches my eye. Then he smiles, and turns back to the crowd. "I'm sorry you're all such a bunch of *losers*.

"Look at you!" Marty shouts. "Blubbering and telling us your pathetic secrets! God—keep it to yourselves! All this blahblah just makes me want to punch you! And these guys"—he jerks his thumb back at the Freakshow—"they're the worst! I mean, Maggie is *insane*. She was in a mental institution—remember that part of the story? She's probably heading back there after this is all over! Right?"

He stands there a moment, like he expects a response. But the crowd is completely silent. Nobody speaks. Nobody moves.

Finally, I step forward. I touch Bloom's shoulder, and he turns to look at me, smiling a hideous smile. I want to hit him. I want to claw at him. I want to scream. I want to say something brilliant and witty and devastating. But, in the end, I say the only thing I can think of.

"Boo," I say.

Bloom laughs. "What?"

"Boo!" Eggy shouts. "Booooooooo!"

"Cut it out, loser," Marty says, but, suddenly, the entire crowd is booing and hissing, and shouting for Bloom to get off the stage. He tries to say something else, but I can't

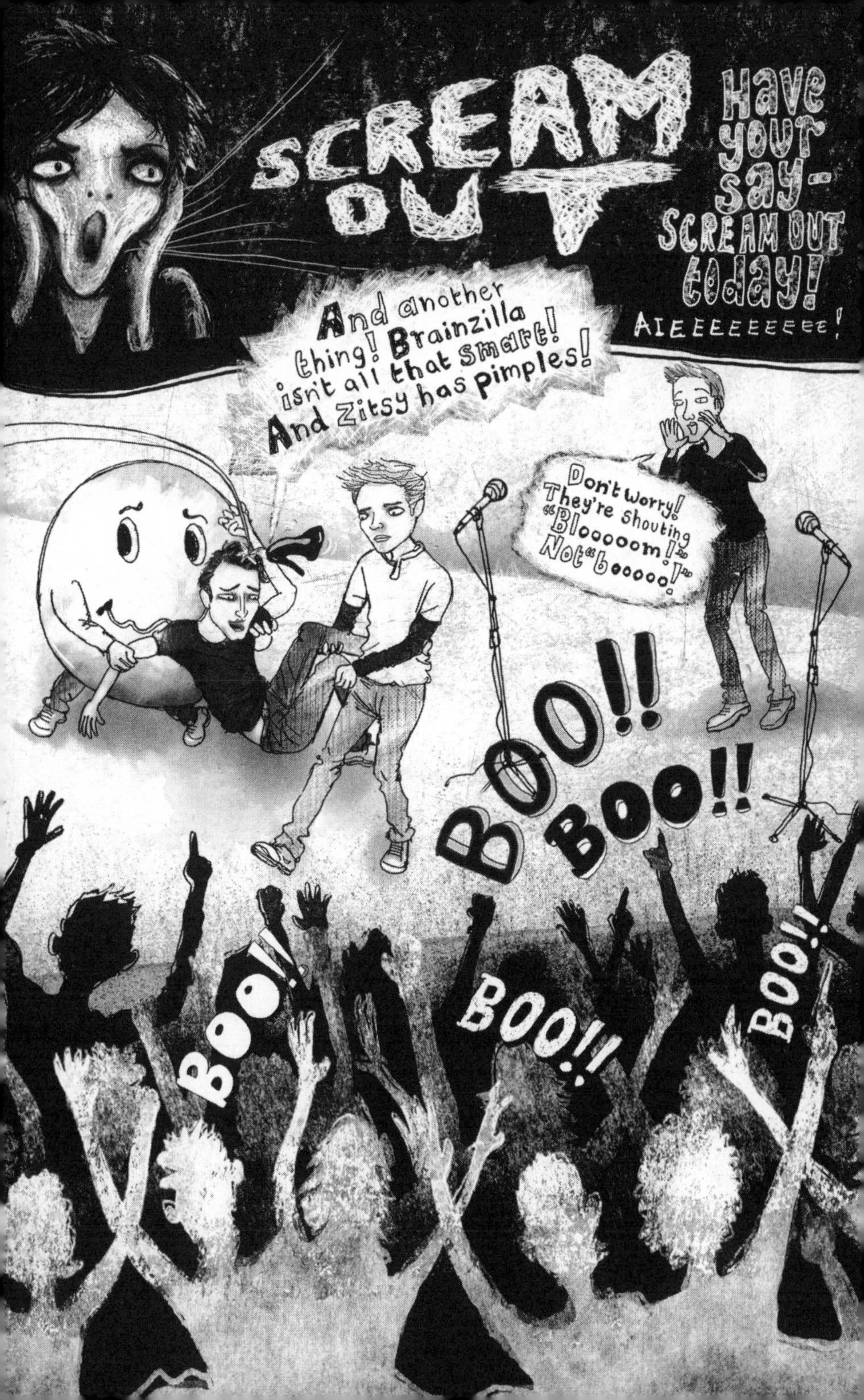
SCREAM OUT
Have your say- SCREAM OUT today!
AIEEEEEEEEE!
And another thing! Brainzilla isn't all that Smart! And Zitsy has pimples!
Don't worry! They're shouting "Blooooom!" Not "booooo!"
BOO!!
BOO!!
BOO!!
BOO!!
BOO!!

hear him—the crowd is too loud. Someone actually throws a shoe at his head. Flatso and Tebow don't need any encouragement—they escort him from the stage.

As I watch Bloom get booed off the stage, I feel both disappointed and relieved, which surprises me. Relieved?

I can give up on him now.

That thought is like a door opening.

He isn't going to change, no matter what I do.

I couldn't change Bloom. And I can't change my mother. The only person I can change…is me.

Wow.

I wonder if I can fly.

Do you know what situational irony is? Ms. Olsson pop-quizzed us on it a couple of weeks ago. It's when you expect one thing to happen, but something completely different happens.

The Scream Out gave me a mini revelation about how I couldn't change people. And then this happened:

Ironic? Or just weird?

Everyone in the class is staring at the chalkboard. Nobody speaks. I think most people are too afraid to ask if she really means it about the pop quizzes. Because—you know—what if she *doesn't*?

But I have to know. "Um, excuse me, Ms. Olsson," I say. "Did you write that on the board? About the pop quizzes?"

"I don't remember calling on you," Ms. Olsson snaps.

I put my hand in the air.

"Yes, Ms. Clarke?" she says, starting the conversation over from the beginning. So I repeat my question.

"Yes, I have written that on the board. It has come to my attention that pop quizzes are a great deal of pressure—perhaps more than necessary. My main objective is to be sure that you are completing and comprehending the reading. So I am instituting a new policy: I will assess your understanding of the reading by gauging your participation in classroom discussion. Every single person in this room is expected to make at least one comment per class. Your grade depends on it." And then she smiles at us.

Tebow makes a low whistling noise, and I realize that Ms. Olsson is serious. This is a bit of a shock to my system. I feel a little like you do when you jump into a cold pool—at first, it takes your breath away. Then you realize that you feel pretty good. Ms. Olsson just wants us to talk about books? I can handle that.

I can *more* than handle it!

Some of the teachers were at the rally, and everyone must have heard about it, because there is definitely a kinder, gentler vibe in school. In math, Mrs. Rosewater gives us a pep talk. Well, sort of. She reads from *Oh, The Places You'll Go!*, which is one of my favorite books. It kind of makes me feel like I'm back in kindergarten…in the best possible way.

"Do you think this is because of the rally?" Brainzilla asks me during PE class, where our dodgeball unit has somehow been converted into a unit where we help one another over a wall, perform trust falls, and work together to untie human knots.

"That or a full moon," I reply, casting a sideways glance at Bloom, who has managed to avoid making eye contact for the entire day. I guess it's the best we can hope for from the Haters. And it's fine with me.

We didn't change what we'd expected to—but we did change something. So I'd give our Operation Happiness an A-minus. And that's not bad.

Chapter 69
GETTING GOOGLY

Studies show that periods of unstructured time lead to periods of greater creativity."

"What do you mean by that?" Ms. Kellerman asks me. Yes, I'm back in her office by executive order.

"Didn't you hear the Google lady?" I ask.

Ms. Kellerman writes something on her yellow pad (probably *subject is hallucinating*), and I explain, "The lady from Google, who came to talk to us last week? The Future Careers Club organized it?"

"Oh," Ms. Kellerman says, scratching out what she had written on the pad.

"She said that everybody at Google gets time to wander around and create or just think or whatever for an hour or so every day. They actually get paid for it. So—that's what my diary is," I explain. "It's just my unstructured brain. It's not for sharing. I can only be relaxed and honest in my diary when I'm sure nobody is going to look at it."

Ms. Kellerman is doodling something on her pad. Then, suddenly, she seems to realize what she's doing. She looks at her goofy little flower doodle for a moment, then looks up at me. "I think I can understand that," she says slowly.

New ending for TRAIL BLAZERS' season

New ending for the Age of DINOSAURS

New ending for LOST

New ending

New ending for Romeo & Juliet

New ending for my REPORT CARD

We sit in silence for a moment. Mr. Tool is still insisting that I come talk to her for an hour a week, and I'm starting to wonder if maybe I should give Ms. Kellerman more of a chance. Maybe if I talk to her a little, she'll see I'm not as crazy as she thinks.

"I'm not going to show you my diary," I tell her, "but maybe I could tell you what I'm thinking, sometimes."

"I just want to help you, Margaret," Ms. Kellerman says. "You've been going through a difficult time. You shouldn't have to do it alone."

And—in that one moment, a space shorter than a second, really—I realize that Ms. Kellerman and Ms. Olsson have been making the same mistake. They've been trying to squeeze my thoughts out of me. But I don't need to be squeezed.

I can just talk.

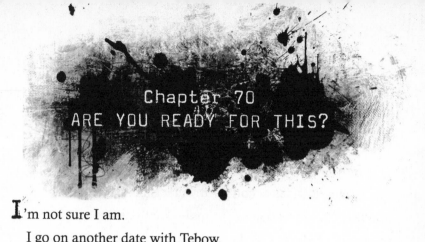

Chapter 70
ARE YOU READY FOR THIS?

I'm not sure I am.

I go on another date with Tebow.

And Laurence.

This time, we go ice-skating. I'm a pretty poor ice-skater, so the whole thing involves a lot of falling over.

"Are you okay?" Tebow asks, reaching for my hand. He pulls me upright, then takes both of my hands in his. "You just have to relax. It's like walking—the more you think about it, the more awkward it is." He begins to skate backward, pulling me with him, and for a while, we're doing pretty well.

"Hey!" I say after a moment, surprised by my forward motion.

"You're doing great," Tebow says, and just then, my skate hits a gouge in the ice and I fall over, taking Tebow with me.

We land on the ice in a heap, but we're both laughing.

Tebow makes me get up and try again, and after about a million more falls, I finally start to get the hang of it. Afterward, we go get hot chocolates from Insomnia Coffee. I'm sitting there with whipped cream on my upper lip, laughing at something Tebow has just said, when I realize, *This is not a date.*

It isn't a date, because I don't want to be on a date with Tebow. I've been trying so hard to figure out what Tebow was thinking that I forgot to think for myself. But here is my thought: If Tebow becomes my boyfriend, we might have to break up someday.

And I never, ever want to break up with any of my best friends.

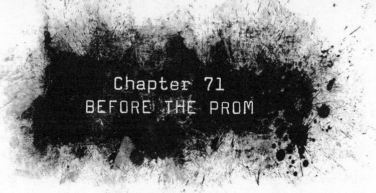

Twirl," Marjorie commands, so I do. When I come full circle, I hardly recognize the girl in the mirror. I feel like I haven't really looked at myself in months. And here I am—in a pale peach tulle dress, with a sparkly barrette in my hair.

I think I've mentioned that Marjorie has some surprising talents.

"Three years sewing costumes for the drama department of a community college," Marjorie says as she fusses with my right sleeve, "come in surprisingly handy. Take it from me—everyone should do it."

"Thank you," I say.

"Oh, I have lots more advice," she tells me.

"I meant—thanks for making me the dress. Although the advice is helpful, too."

Marjorie seems surprised and pleased at the compliment. Her wild hair is held back by a headband, and I can see her face. She looks a lot like Mrs. Morris. That shouldn't be surprising, but it is.

Marjorie gives me a hug. "It's my pleasure, Cuckoo," she whispers.

She finished just in time, because ten minutes later, the

Freakshow is at my front door. They've pulled up in a limo (a gift from Eggy's parents).

I have to say that all my friends look incredibly beautiful. Even Zitsy looks gorgeous, although how he is managing that in a powder-blue tuxedo is a mystery for the ages. Brainzilla is wearing white. Not the Vera Wang wedding dress, but close. Flatso is wearing midnight-blue velvet and looks like a goddess. Tebow is predictably handsome. And Eggy is wearing a vibrant, anime-inspired sequin gown that looks like it came straight out of Lady Gaga's closet.

"Everyone line up in front of the limo!" Marjorie shouts, holding up an expensive-looking camera with a long lens.

"She spent six months working as a photographer's assistant," I explain to my friends. But the Freakshow doesn't need an explanation.

"Got it!" Marjorie hugs every single one of us, and we get into the limo. Our driver, Earl, is friendly, but not too chatty. I have to say, the limo is really cool inside. It has a TV and a mini fridge and huge seats that are as comfortable as the ones in Mr. Tool's office.

"Earl, is it okay if I open the sunroof?" I ask.

"Everybody does," he says, and the roof opens with a low hum.

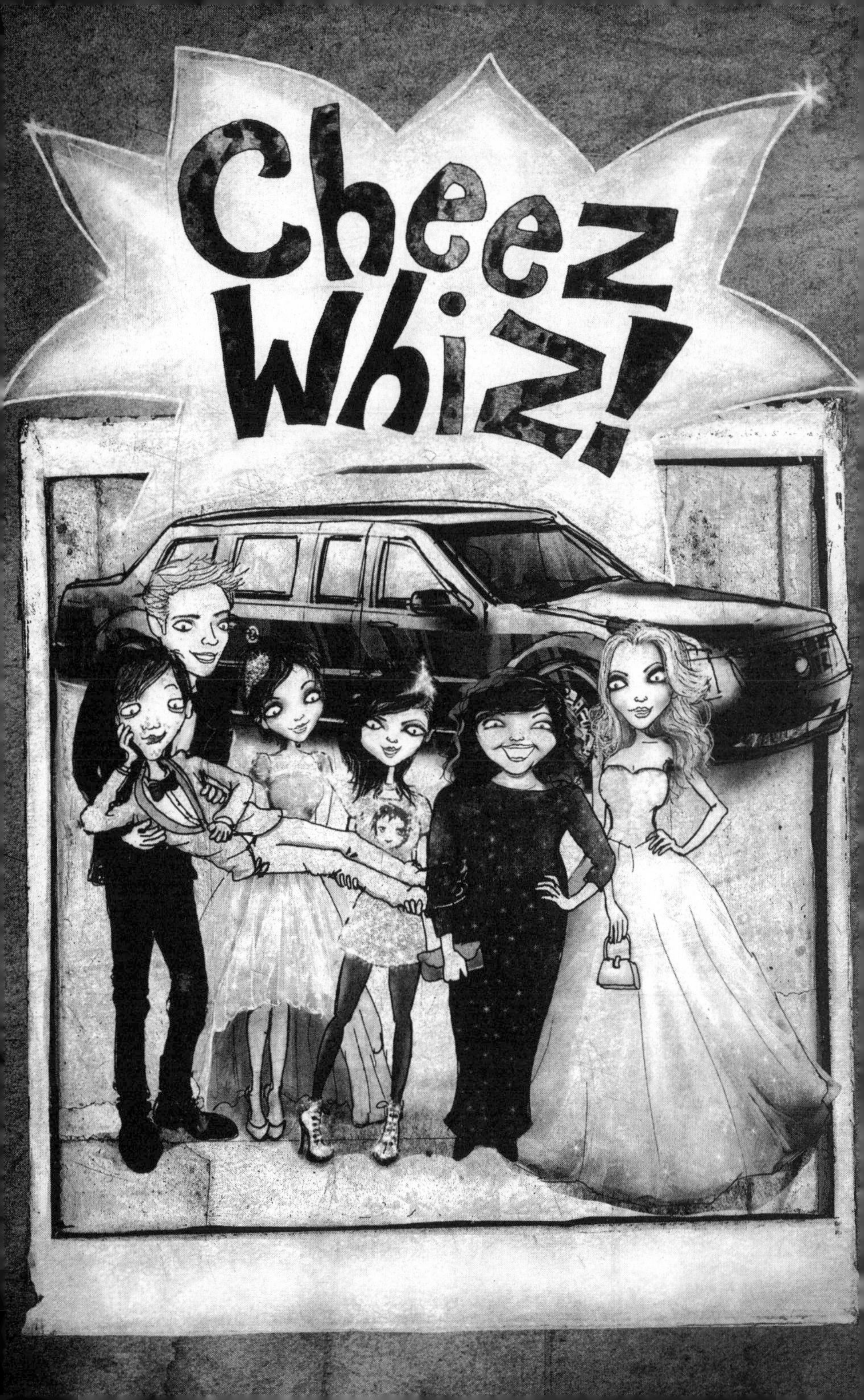
Cheez Whiz!

I Know this has been in a jillion movies. It's even more fun than it looks!

We pull up to the Holiday Inn and head to the room where our school has set up the Back to the Millennium Prom. Well, that's the official name.

Unofficially, though, everyone calls it the Hugs. Would we have come together without the Scream Out? I don't know. But I do know one thing: The Hugs is very emotional. Except for the fistfight between Jacob Answar and Bobby Dupree, it's nothing but love all around.

The Nations have finally come together.

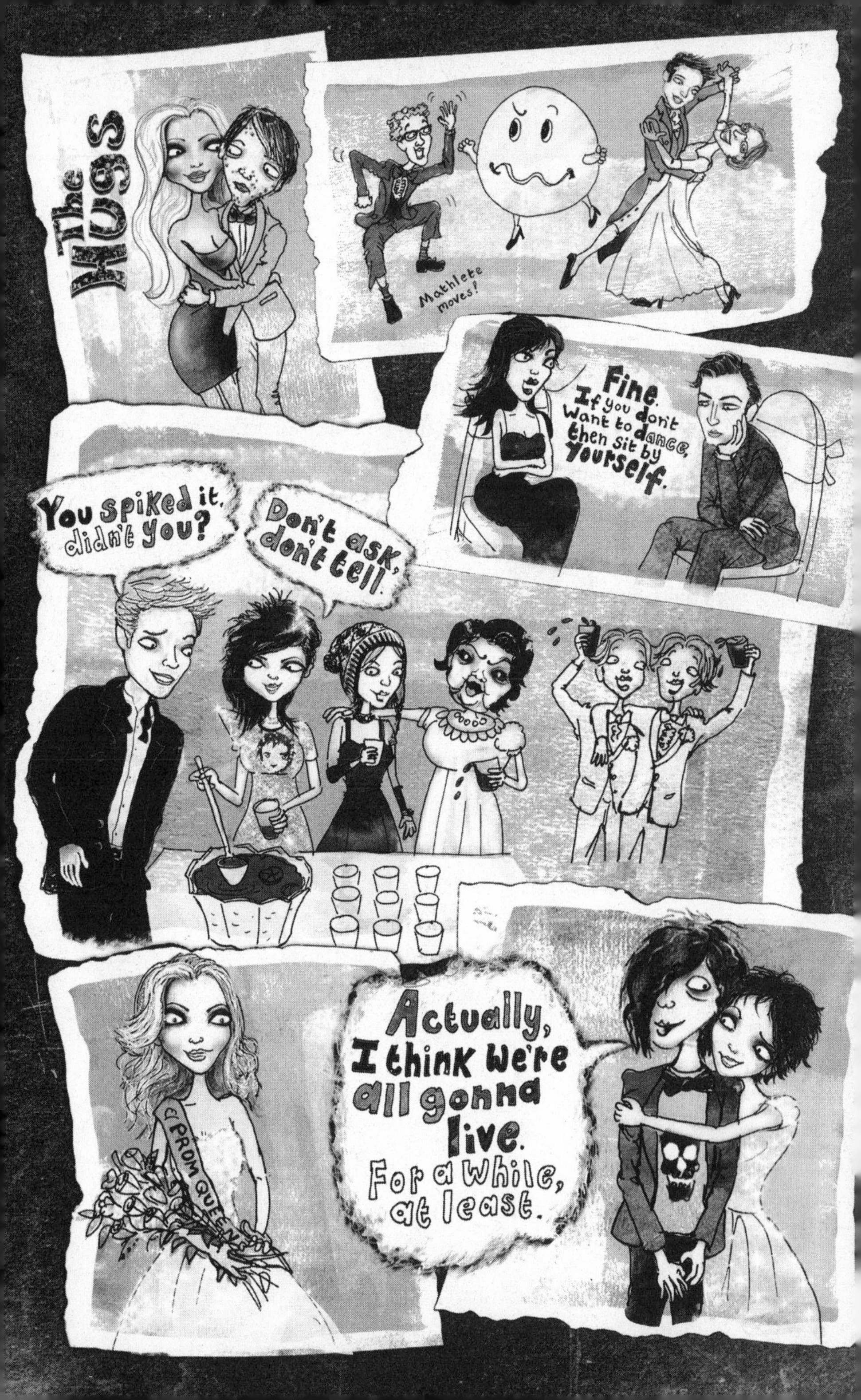
The Hugs
Mathlete moves!
Fine. If you don't want to dance, then sit by yourself.
You spiked it, didn't you?
Don't ask, don't tell.
PROM QUEEN
Actually, I think we're all gonna live. For a while, at least.

And, after it's all over, my friends and I gather at our table.

Brainzilla seems almost hypnotized by the disco ball. "This has been really amazing," she murmurs.

Tebow gives me a shy smile. He had asked me to be his date to the prom, but we decided that it would be better if the whole Freakshow went as friends. I'm really glad we did it that way.

"I'm kind of starting to like these people," Zitsy announces, draining his punch. "Man, this stuff is gooooooood." He stands up. "I love you guys!" he shouts.

Everyone ignores him.

"That's enough punch for you." Eggy takes his glass.

Zitsy turns to her. "I love you."

"I love you, too, Zitsy," she says. He grabs her in a sudden hug. Eggy is surprised, but she just laughs and hugs him back. Then Flatso joins the hug. Then Brainzilla and Tebow. I'm the last...but that's just because I want to wrap them all in my arms.

I just know we'll be friends for the rest of our lives. No matter how long that is.

Chapter 72
TALKING TO MRS. MORRIS

I was the last to get picked up, and I'm the last one left in the limo on our way home.

"Hey, Earl?" I say as we head down Whittaker Avenue. "Would it be okay if we make an extra stop?"

"Fee's paid for eight hours," Earl says over his shoulder. "It has only been six. I'll stop any place you want."

So I give him the directions. I know it's late, but there's someone I really want to visit.

"Marjorie's my housemate now. We're actually a really good match. I can see why you were proud of her. She's got a lot of amazing talents. She made me this dress. Can you believe that?" I talk to Mrs. Morris for a while—probably more that night than I ever did in real life. We were used to comfortable silence. But there are a few things I want her to know. Things I want to say out loud.

"School is a lot better. Either my teachers are getting nicer or else I'm getting used to them. And Tebow—well, you always said he was a nice boy. He is. But I still miss you. I love you, Mom. I hope you don't mind it if I call you that. But that's who you were to me. Who you are. And who you'll always be."

Chapter 73
WINNING

Ding-dong.

It's Sunday, two days after the end of school. I have no idea who could be dropping by at nine in the morning, but I figure it's probably not an ax murderer, so I put down my diary and shout, "I'll get it!"

That wasn't really necessary, since Marjorie is still asleep and Morris the Dog is already barking madly. I pull a linty treat from my pocket and toss it to him. I wait until he's trotting happily toward the couch before I pull open the door.

It takes me a minute to even realize who it is. Winnie Quinn is wearing jeans, which make him look like the teenager he is.

"H-h-hi," I stammer. I'm too shocked to be very coherent.

"Hi, Kooks," he says.

It hits me that I am still in my pajamas and that my hair is very likely doing an impersonation of a bird's nest right now. But I'm pretty sure I can't close the door and try this over again, so we stare at each other a moment. Finally, I think of something to say. "Do you want to come in?"

"Actually, I can't stay long. I just wanted to let you know that I'm not coming back to North Plains High School next year. I

got a research job at Portland State, so I'm going to be working over there."

"Uh—congratulations."

He nods. "I'm pretty excited about it. Anyway, I'm not going to be your teacher anymore. I'm not going to be a teacher at all."

I'm not sure how to respond. *Too bad? You were good? It's a loss to the profession?* In the end, what comes out of my mouth is "I'll miss you."

Winnie turns pink. "Well…I, uh—I wondered if you might want to go to the movies sometime. With me." He laughs like he's embarrassed.

I admit it. I'm floored. "You want to take me to the movies?"

He hesitates, and I realize I might have totally read this wrong. It's Tebow all over again. *He just wants to be friends, you nutty Cuckoo—*

"Yes. I want to take you to the movies. Sorry. I'm not very good at this. It's just that...you're really beautiful, Margaret."

"You're really beautiful, too," I say finally. I have no idea where that came from. *Stop talking!* I command myself, which does not work at all, because I immediately add, "Would this be a date?"

"Um…" Winnie turns bright pink.

"Scratch that," I say quickly. "Forget I said it. We'll figure it out later."

He looks slightly—only slightly—relieved, but still embarrassed. Which is how I'm feeling, too. Why does this stuff always have to be so awkward?

My hand is holding open the door, and Winnie puts his fingers over mine. Very gently. His hand is warm. "Will you call me?"

"Yes," I promise.

"Good." And then, after giving me a slip of paper with his number scrawled on it, he walks away. I watch his retreating form, wondering if it was all a dream. And I'm struck by the idea that I may really, truly fall in love with Winnie Quinn in the actual world, not just in my mind.

Chapter 74
TEBOW'S PREFERRED ENDING

As you may have noticed, I'm into alternate endings. Here's one for Tebow.

Chapter 75
ZITSY'S ENDING

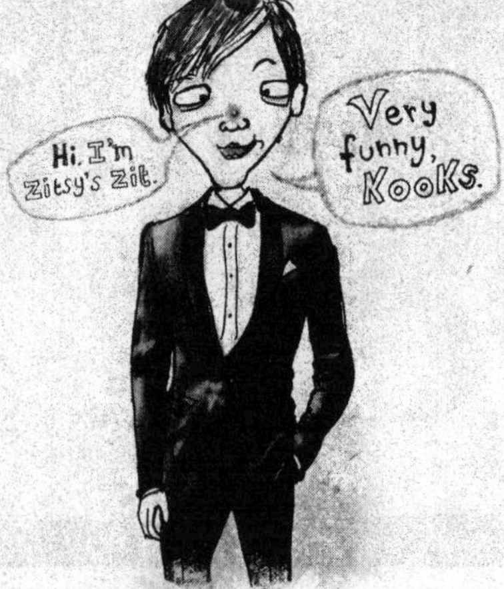
Hi, I'm Zitsy's Zit.
Very funny, Kooks.

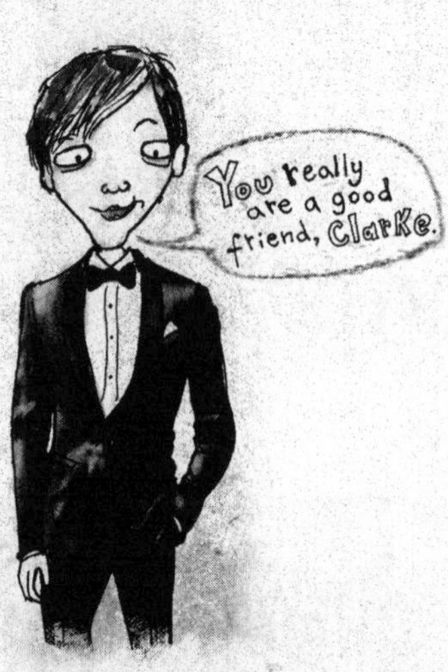
You really are a good friend, Clarke.

Chapter 76

BRAINZILLA, EGGY, AND FLATSO'S ENDING

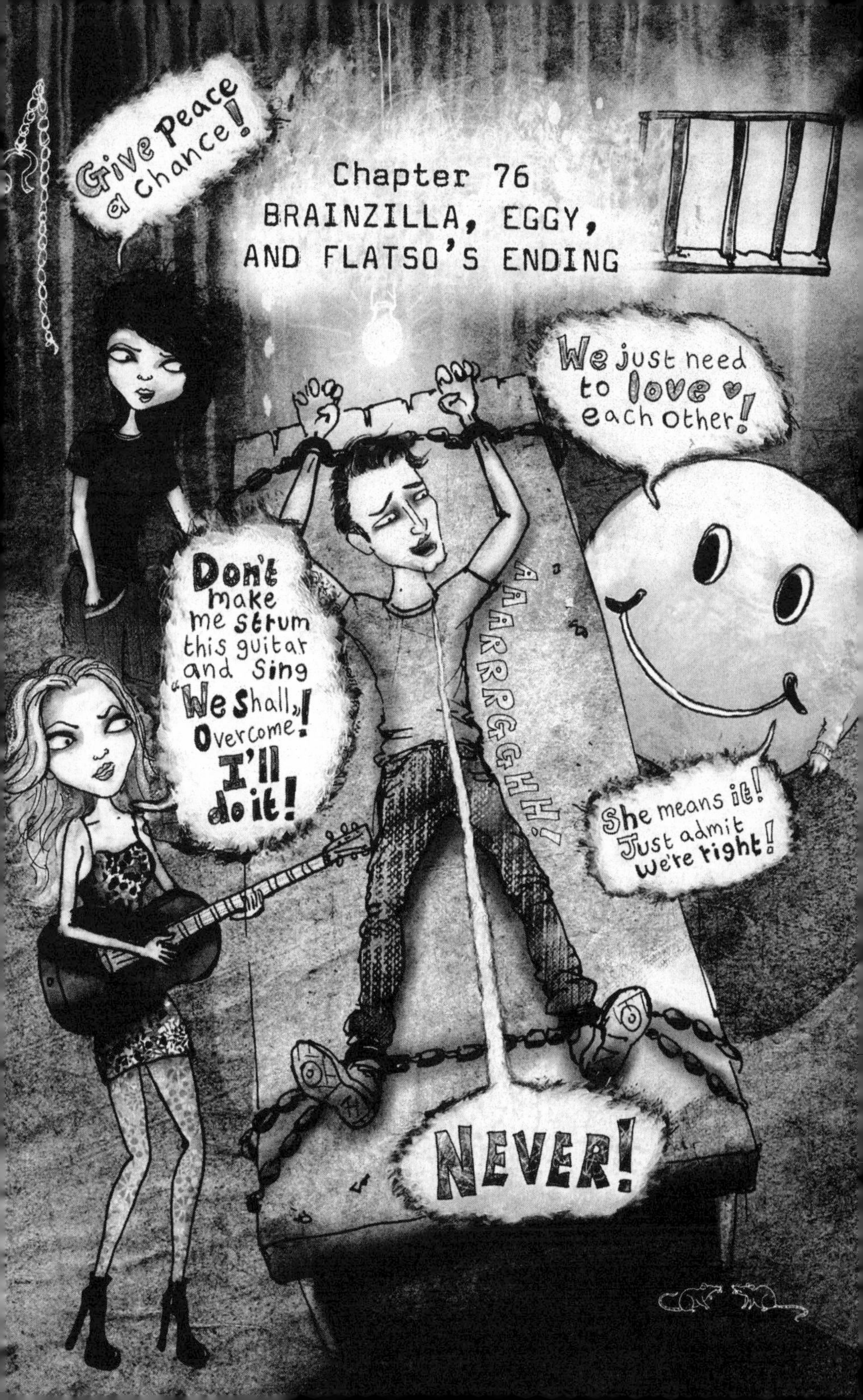

Give Peace a Chance!
We just need to love each other!
Don't make me strum this guitar and sing "We Shall Overcome"! I'll do it!
AAARRRGGHH!
She means it! Just admit we're right!
NEVER!

Chapter 77
BYE

And finally, finally, here's my alternate ending for the Twilight series.

Apologies to Ms. Meyer.

Dearest Edward,

You know that I love the way we can stare into each other's eyes for hours and hours, and you know that I love how we talk so softly that no one else can understand what we're saying, but I've been thinking deeply about this — about us — and, Edward, I can't have babies with little red eyes and sharp, pointy incisors. And I don't think I can be with you for eternity — not if it means running through the woods at night and eating squirrels. And possibly deer. It would be different if we could cook them first. So I have to say good-bye, dearest Edward. It's better this way, my dearest, my sweetest love of my life. Good-bye.

Edward as Edward Cullen

Me as Bella Swan

What do you think?

And for you, you don't get off so easily. I love writing in this diary—to you. And I don't really like endings. They always seem so final.

Besides, I'll have to tell you about what happens with Winnie.

You'll probably want to meet my mom...when she shows up. We'll both want to hear her seamy side of the story, am I right?

I'll have to give you the update on Tebow.

And you'll need to know everything the Freakshow gets into. Thrills and chills, tears and fears, chuckles and gerfuckles. (That's Brainzilla's word. Not sure if it's obscene or not, but this is my diary, so I'm leaving it in.)

Plus, I have this incredible new alternate beginning for Beethoven's Fifth Symphony.

So, good-bye.

For now.

This isn't an ending! I don't do endings!

A Note to Our Readers

If you're experiencing emotional or physical abuse, or having difficulty dealing with your anxiety, your anger, or other negative emotions, you don't have to handle it alone. Talking to a trusted adult, a family doctor, or a counselor is the first step toward finding help for your problems.

Approaching an adult in your life for help isn't an option for everyone. If you'd like to speak privately to someone who is trained to listen to what you're feeling, please check out these resources below. They can find you the support you need in any situation that is bringing you down, no matter how big or small your problems are.

Childhelp National Child Abuse Hotline
1-800-422-4453 or childhelp.org for more information
For support in any abusive situation, including bullying, cyberbullying, and emotional or physical abuse

National Alliance on Mental Illness
1-800-950-6264 for information on mental health issues and referrals to local support groups
Also visit strengthofus.org for an online community for young adults affected by mental health issues

National Suicide Prevention Lifeline
1-800-273-8255 or suicidepreventionlifeline.org for live chat
For support if you are at a low point and are thinking of hurting yourself

DELIVER US FROM EVIL

Two teenagers claim that they're pregnant.
And *virgins*.

One is carrying the son of God—
and the other is carrying the son of Satan.

CRADLE *and* ALL

JAMES PATTERSON

Turn the page for a shocking sneak peek…

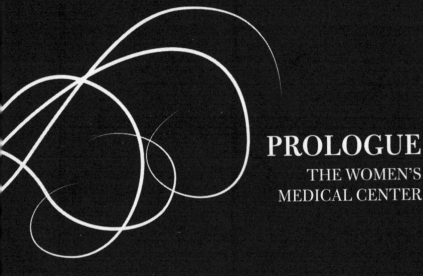

PROLOGUE
THE WOMEN'S
MEDICAL CENTER

Sundown had bloodied the horizon over the uneven rooftops of South Boston. Birds were perched on every roof, and they seemed to be watching the girl walking slowly below.

Kathleen Beavier made her way down a shadowy side street that was as alien to her as the surface of the moon. She hunched her shoulders and pulled up the collar on her vintage peacoat. Her black Frye boots had rubbed raw circles into her heels, but she welcomed the pain. It was a distraction from the unthinkable thing she had come to do.

This is so unreal, so impossible, she thought. *So completely insane.*

The seventeen-year-old girl paused to catch her breath at the intersection of Dorchester and Broadway. South Boston wasn't really rough anymore, not the way it used to be, but she still didn't look as if she belonged here. She was too preppy, despite the tough boots. Just a bit too pretty and golden and polished.

That was her plan, though. She'd never bump into anyone she knew in Southie.

With badly shaking hands, Kathleen pushed the tortoiseshell sunglasses she didn't need anymore back into her blond hair. She'd washed it earlier with Bumble and bumble shampoo and rinsed it with conditioner. But why, really? How ridiculous to have worried about how her damn hair would look.

She squeezed her eyes shut and uttered a long, hopeless moan of confusion and despair.

When Kathleen finally forced open her eyes, she blinked into the slashing red rays of the setting sun. Then she checked the time on her iPhone for the millionth time in the past hour.

God, no. It's already past five!

She was late for her doctor's appointment.

She started to run. She hurried past the imposing brick face of St. Augustine's parish church, past a neon-lit dive bar and a dusty florist's shop. A man on a motorcycle called out, "Blondie, what's the rush? Can I get a smile?"

She whipped herself forward, as she often did to protect herself against the New England winter. Tears ran down her cheeks, warm trails that soon turned cold.

Hurry, hurry. You have to do this terrible thing. You've come this far.

It was already twenty after the hour when she finally found what she was looking for. The gray brick building was wedged in between a twenty-four-hour laundromat and a diner with steamed-up windows.

This is the place. This . . . hellhole.

The walls were smeared with lipstick-red and black graffiti: *Abortion = Murder. Abortion Is the Unforgivable Sin.* There was a glass door and beside it a tarnished brass plaque: WOMEN'S MEDICAL CENTER, it read.

Sorrow washed over her and she felt faint. She didn't want to go through with it. She wasn't sure she could.

But she made herself walk through the front door. Inside, the reception room was calming, almost reassuring. Pastel-colored plastic chairs ringed the perimeter, and posters of sweet-faced mothers and chubby babies hung on the walls. Best of all, no one was here.

Kathleen took a clipboard left out on a countertop. A sign instructed her to fill out the form as best she could.

She sat in a powder-blue chair and began writing down her medical history in block letters. Her hands were shaking harder now. Her foot wouldn't stop tapping.

What is the reason for today's visit? the form asked.

Kathleen probed her memory for something—anything—that would help her make sense of her situation. She came up with nothing.

This can't be happening to me, she thought. *I shouldn't be in the Women's Medical Center.*

She'd made out with guys, but damn it, damn it, *damn it,* she knew the difference between kissing and...fucking.

She'd never gone all the way with anyone. She hadn't wanted to.

Not that she'd signed a purity pledge or anything like that. She just...hadn't found someone she liked enough. Trusted enough. Did that make her a prude? No, it made her *discerning.*

She'd never even let a guy touch her down there.

The tests must have been wrong, because it wasn't physically possible for them to be right. Like her dad always said, Kathleen Beavier was a good kid, the best. She was popular. She was everybody's friend.

She was a virgin.

But she was pregnant.

A sudden wave of nausea came over Kathleen and nearly knocked her to the floor. She felt dizzy and thought she might throw up in the waiting room.

"Get yourself together," she said softly. *You're not the first one to go through this kind of thing. You won't be the last, either.*

She glanced at the clock over the vacant reception desk. It was nearly six. Where was the receptionist? More important, where was the doctor?

Kathleen wanted to turn around and run out of the women's clinic, but she fought off the powerful instinct. But where *was* everybody?

"You can do this," she said between clenched teeth. "No time like the present."

Kathleen stood and walked to a pinewood door behind the reception desk. She took a deep breath, possibly the deepest of her life. She turned the metal handle, and the door opened.

She heard a soft, mellow voice coming from down the hall. *Thank God, someone's here after all.*

She followed the sound.

"Hello," Kathleen called out tentatively. "Hello? Anybody? I'm Kathleen Beavier. I have an appointment."

The door at the far end of the hall was partially open, and Kathleen heard the pleasing voice inside. She slowly pushed the door open all the way.

"Hello?"

Something was wrong—she sensed it instantly. Kathleen felt she should leave, *right now,* but it had taken so much courage to come here in the first place.

The air seemed thick, almost viscous. There was a smell of alcohol. But something else, too—something metallic and heavy. Kathleen put her hand to her mouth.

It took her a few seconds to take in the full horror of what she saw.

A young, dark-haired woman was hanging from a hook high up on the wall. She wore a white medical coat. Her name tag read DR. HIGGINS. A cord was slipknotted tightly around her neck.

Her once pretty face was a brutal dark red, and her eyes were frozen open in fear. Her brown hair cascaded over her shoulders.

Trembling, Kathleen reached out and touched the woman's hand. It was still warm.

Dr. Higgins. Her doctor.

In a panic, Kathleen jerked her arm away. She wanted to run, but some force held her there. Something so powerful. So awful.

She saw a stethoscope coiled beside a pad of paper. On the pad was written Kathleen's name. Her stomach twisted. Fear and guilt and shame overpowered her in one sickening, wrenching ache.

The idea that came to her next was so strange, so overwhelming, it was almost as if it weren't her own.

Enough, she thought. *I have had enough.*

A tray of instruments glittered near the pad of paper. Kathleen took up a sharp blade. It was ice-cold and menacing in her hand.

She heard a voice—but no one was there. The Voice was deep, commanding. *You know what you have to do, Kathleen. We've talked about it. Go ahead, now. It's the right thing.*

She didn't question it. In the space between the pink sleeve of her Kate Spade oxford shirt and the crease of her left wrist, she sliced. The skin parted.

See how easy it is, Kathleen? It's nothing, really. Just the natural order of things.

Blood welled up and fell in large drops onto the floor. Tears flowed from her eyes, mixing with the blood.

One more cut. Just to be sure.

The second cut was harder for her to do. Her pretty gold cuff bracelet covered the best place on her vein, and her left hand was already weak.

She sliced into the vein again.

She sank to her knees, as if in prayer.

Kathleen managed a third slash before everything jumped to black.

She fell unconscious beneath the feet of the hanging doctor, whose mouth now seemed curved in a knowing smile.

READ MORE IN

ABOUT THE AUTHORS AND ILLUSTRATOR

JAMES PATTERSON holds the Guinness World Record for the most #1 *New York Times* bestsellers, including *Middle School* and *I Funny*. He is a tireless champion of the power of books and reading, exemplified by his new children's book imprint, JIMMY Patterson, whose mission is simple: We want every kid who finishes a JIMMY Book to say: "PLEASE GIVE ME ANOTHER BOOK." He has donated more than one million books to students and soldiers and has over four hundred Teacher Education Scholarships at twenty-four colleges and universities. He has also donated millions to independent bookstores and school libraries. James will be investing his proceeds from the sales of JIMMY Patterson Books in pro-reading initiatives.

LISA PAPADEMETRIOU is the author of the Confectionately Yours series and many other novels for young adults. She has also collaborated with James Patterson on *Middle School: Big Fat Liar*. She lives in Massachusetts with her family.

KEINO are a British illustration team whose artwork has been featured in books and exhibitions across the UK and Europe. They are currently locked in their remote mountain studio, writing and illustrating their debut young adult novel.